Christmas in Paradise

AMISH BY ACCIDENT TRILOGY

J. E. B. Spredemann

Blessed Publishing

BOOKS BY J.E.B. SPREDEMANN
(*J. Spredemann)

AMISH GIRLS SERIES

Joanna's Struggle

Danika's Journey

Chloe's Revelation

Susanna's Surprise

Annie's Decision

Abigail's Triumph

Brooke's Quest

Leah's Legacy

NOVELLAS*

*Amish by Accident**

An Unforgivable Secret - Amish Secrets 1*

A Secret Encounter - Amish Secrets 2*

A Secret of the Heart - Amish Secrets 3*

An Undeniable Secret - Amish Secrets 4*

Learning to Love – Saul's Story (Sequel to Chloe's Revelation – adult novella)*

A Christmas of Mercy – Amish Girls Holiday

*Englisch on Purpose (Prequel to Amish by Accident)**

Christmas in Paradise – (Final book in Amish by Accident trilogy)

To those struggling to hold on to a failing marriage, don't give up!

God is still in the business of miracles.

Author's Note

It should be noted that the Amish/Mennonite people and their communities differ one from another. There are, in fact, no two Amish communities exactly alike. It is this premise on which this book is written. We have taken cautious steps to assure the authenticity of Amish practices and customs. New Order Amish and Mennonites are portrayed in this work of fiction and may differ from some communities.

We, as *Englischers*, can learn a lot from the Plain People and their simple way of life. Their hard work, close-knit family life, and concern for others are to be applauded. As the Lord wills, may this special culture continue to be respected and remain so for many centuries to come, and may the light of God's salvation reach their hearts.

Characters in *Christmas in Paradise*

The Greene Family
Richard – Mattie's husband, protagonist, character in *Englisch on Purpose*
Mattie (Riehl) – Protagonist, main character in *Englisch on Purpose*
Lizzy and Matthew – Richard and Mattie's children

The Welch Family
Carson – Elisabeth's husband, character in *Amish by Accident*
Elisabeth (Schrock) – Protagonist of *Amish by Accident*
Lincoln, Jacob, Benjamin, and Leah – Carson and Elisabeth's children

The Schrock Family
Jacob – Elisabeth's younger brother, Rachel's husband, character in *Amish by Accident*
Rachel (Brenneman) – Jacob's wife, daughter of Saul and Chloe, character in *Amish by Accident*

The Riehl Family
Matthew – Maryanna's husband, character in *Englisch on Purpose*, *A Christmas of Mercy*, and the *Amish Girls Series* (best friend of Jonathan Fisher)

Maryanna (Hostettler) – Mattie's mother, daughter of Judah (bishop), character in *Englisch on Purpose*, *A Christmas of Mercy*, and the *Amish Girls Series*

The Fisher Family
Jonathan – main character throughout the *Amish Girls Series*, minister
JJ (Johnny and Judah) – twin sons of Jonathan and Susanna, cousins and good friends of Mattie

The Beiler Family
Brianna – Luke's wife, protagonist in *Amish by Accident*
Luke – Brianna's husband, main character in *Amish by Accident*

Unofficial Glossary
of Pennsylvania Dutch Words

Ach – Oh

Boppli – Baby

Dat/Daed – Dad

Denki – Thanks

Der Herr – The Lord

Dochder – Daughter

Englischer – A non-Amish person

Fraa – Woman, Wife

Gott – God

Gut – Good

Hullo – Hello

Jah – Yes

Kinner – Children

Kinskinner – Grandchildren

Mamm – Mom

Schatzi – Honey, Sweetheart

Vatter – Father

ONE

Carson squinted as he turned into the country lane, the rays of the sun reflecting off his Volvo's platinum hood. He moved his sunglasses from his head to his eyes, quickly putting an end to his momentary blindness. The second he spotted the farmhouse, a smile danced on his lips. Just as he'd thought, his beautiful wife, Elisabeth, had come out to greet him, their two oldest children stationed at each leg.

The minute he stepped out of the vehicle, their oldest son was tugging on his pant leg. "Daddy, Daddy!"

Carson shifted his gaze from his wife to his son. "What are you so excited about, Lincoln?"

"Mommy showed me how to spell my name today. L-i-n-c-o-" He paused momentarily, an unsure expression crossed his face, and he looked up at his mother. Elisabeth nodded in affirmation. "-l-n?"

"That's right. Very good." Carson tousled the boy's hair and swept him up into his arms.

J. E. B. Spredemann

"That's not all. Mommy said just three more weeks till Christmas!"

"Three weeks? Is that all?"

Lincoln nodded his head profusely. "And *Dawdi* Ben and *Mammi* Leah are coming to visit! And cousins too."

Carson's brow raised as he and Elisabeth met gazes. "I thought we were going to the city to visit Mattie and Richard."

Elisabeth glanced at the children and raised a half-smile. "Change of plans. Let's talk about it after supper."

Carson understood her meaning. She didn't wish to discuss the situation in the children's presence. Hopefully everything was okay with Richard and Mattie.

He released Lincoln from his embrace once they were inside the house and instructed the children to go play in the living room. Carson followed Elisabeth into the kitchen. "Mm... smells good. What are you making?"

She peeked into the oven, then quickly shut the door. "Pizza."

"Vegan pizza?" His lips twisted.

"*Jah*. I found a recipe online today and decided to try it out." She placed a potholder on the counter.

"Sounds great." Carson reached for her hand and drew her close. "So, what's going on with Mattie and Richard?" He kissed her forehead.

He read something in Elisabeth's expression. Was it sadness? Worry? "It's not good, Carson." Her bottom lip quivered. "I think they may be getting a divorce."

2

Carson wiped the tear that slipped down her cheek. "A divorce? Why?"

She shrugged. "Mattie thinks Richard's seeing someone else. She's pretty certain."

Carson shook his head in disbelief.

Elisabeth continued on. "She said they haven't been going to church lately, and after she had little Matthew, life just got busy."

"We should go see them."

Elisabeth searched his eyes. "Promise me, Carson, that you won't ever leave me."

Carson held her close and allowed her to release as many tears as she needed. "I promised you that the day we married, and I don't ever intend to break that promise." He lifted her chin until he caught her eye. "Do you hear me?"

At her nod, he bent down and pressed his lips to hers. "I love you and I always will," he whispered reassuringly. "Don't ever doubt that."

Mattie glanced down at the envelope in her hand and wiped away the tears that cascaded down her cheeks. If only she'd heeded her father's warnings years ago. Oh, how she missed home! The thought of returning both thrilled and frightened her. What would Dad say when he learned that she'd named his grandson after him? He'd be shocked, for sure and certain.

She'd been content in New York until...*until when?* She thought for a moment and tried to pinpoint exactly when she'd lost her joy. Had it been when Elisabeth and Carson moved to the country?

Mattie glanced over at the bookshelf and her cranberry-colored Bible caught her eye. How long had it been since she'd removed it from the shelf and meditated on the words inside? A dull ache tugged at her heart but she couldn't drag herself over to the bookshelf. Not now, when she was angry at God. How could He allow Richard to leave her and their children? Why hadn't He stopped him?

A vision flashed in her mind and her tears came rushing to the surface once again. How many times had she relived this scene in her mind? How many times did Richard's guilt-ridden eyes meet hers as his fingers interlaced with his secretary's?

"Mattie, I can explain," he'd said.

But no explanation was needed. She'd known it in her heart for quite some time now. She and Richard had been drifting apart. He'd become distant. He'd been 'working' longer hours. Their relationship had begun a downward spiral and it seemed every time they spoke to each other it ended in an argument. Some days, he didn't even come home.

Richard had pled with her to see their pastor for counseling, but she refused. Their pastor was a man, so naturally he'd side with Richard. She knew she'd be blamed for every problem they had. And surely Richard would blame their dearth of intimacy for his wandering eye. Had she been the perfect wife, they wouldn't have any of these problems. Quarreling with her husband was bad enough. She wasn't about to carry more guilt on her shoulders than she already had.

Mattie's eyes drifted toward the window where a fresh dusting of snow lined the corners. Oh, to go back to the days when she and Richard were in love! She recalled the time they'd gone ice skating in Central Park and he caught her just before she landed on the ice. The young boy whizzing by her probably had no idea he'd knocked her off her feet. She'd been ice skating many times but not with so many other people. The private ponds where she'd ice skated in Paradise as a child and teen were never as crowded as the city ice skating rinks.

Another tug at her heart compelled Mattie to return home. She nodded and reached for a pen and blank notebook paper. If one of her parents responded to her letter, she would go. How would Mom and Dad react when meeting their grandchildren for the first time? What would her folks say when only she and the children returned home? There's no doubt they'd ask about Richard. Should she bare her soul and spill the whole ugly truth? Perhaps it would be best to just say Richard stayed in the city and leave it at that. If they asked any more questions, she could tell them it was none of their business.

But that would be disrespectful, wouldn't it? Mattie shook her head. Wow, she really *had* changed. Since when had she ever cared about respecting her parents? She owed much to God for her growth. And to Richard, she realized. Where on earth did they go wrong?

After addressing the envelope, she pondered how this Christmas would affect the children. They were still young, but celebrating the most wonderful time of the year without their father present would surely ring alarm in their fragile young minds. To them, their grandparents would be as strangers. She would be their only source of stability and security.

She wondered how long they would stay in Paradise. Would they leave after the holidays or would they stay longer? Of course, that all depended on how she and Dad got along. Maybe she would end up not staying at all. It would be strange entering her childhood home with most of her siblings now gone.

Did Rebekah have any children? Before Elisabeth left the Amish, she'd informed Mattie that her sister Rebekah had a beau. Surely they would have married by now. And what of her other siblings? Were any of them married?

For better or worse, she'd probably find out soon.

TWO

Elisabeth hung up the phone after several attempts to reach Mattie. Where was she? She'd left a message yesterday on both her home phone and her cell phone to no avail. Had she and Richard gone somewhere?

"Carson, I'm worried about Mattie. I can't get a hold of her."

Carson set the newspaper down and looked at Elisabeth. "I can try Richard."

"Would you?"

"Sure, but he's often difficult to get a hold of so don't get your hopes up."

"I won't."

Carson pulled out his cell phone. His brow rose. "Richard?"

Elisabeth could hear Richard's brief response. "Yes. Is this Carson?"

"It is. Listen, Lis has been trying to get a hold of Mattie for the last couple of days. Do you know where she is?"

Elisabeth couldn't make out Richard's reply this time.

"How long has it been since you've seen her?" Carson frowned. "Oh. Well, if you talk to her, will you tell her Elisabeth is trying to get a hold of her?"

Carson looked at Elisabeth. "And Richard, I just want to let you know that we're praying for you."

Elisabeth waited until Carson's call was finished. "Well?"

"He hasn't seen her since last week." Carson frowned.

"Last week?" Elisabeth shook her head.

"He did sound concerned and said he would stop by the house." Carson slipped his cell phone back in to his pants pocket.

"Is he going to call you back?"

"He said he'd tell Mattie you called. I'm guessing she'll be the one calling back."

"Did he say anything else?"

"Not really." Carson blew out a breath.

"When was he going to stop by the house?"

"He didn't say, Lis. But I'm guessing he'll do it today."

"I should hope so."

Carson reached for her hand and squeezed it gently. "Let's just pray for them, okay?"

Elisabeth nodded, tears stinging her eyes.

"Lis, it'll all work out. You'll see."

"You can't know that, Carson."

"No, but I know Richard and Mattie. And I know God. Let's leave it in His hands. He's more than able." Carson's mouth turned up and he pulled her close. "Just look at us. He took a restless Amish girl and placed her right into the arms of a lonely city boy."

She smiled. "Who now lives on a farm."

"And loves every minute of it." Carson bent down and met her lips. "By the way, where are the children?"

"Ours or theirs?"

"Ours. Hopefully theirs are with their mother."

"The baby's sleeping in the nursery with her brother and the two oldest were outside on the swing set last time I checked." She broke away, to his obvious disappointment. "Which reminds me, I should check on them again."

Elisabeth walked to the window to peek out at the backyard. Just last year, Carson, with the help of Saul Brenneman, had enclosed a small covered area so the children could be protected from the harsh elements. He'd said it was to provide her with sanity when the children became restless from being cooped up inside during the winter months. Elisabeth thought it had been a genius idea. She now smiled as Lincoln pushed Jacob on the swing. How happy her children seemed.

A pang of regret seared her heart as she thought of Mattie and Richard's children. What must they be thinking right now? Did they know their young lives were about to be shattered by the enemy of their souls? How horrible divorce must be for the innocent ones who had little understanding. If only Mattie and Richard would consider their children's futures and the devastating consequences a decision of this magnitude would bring upon them.

Mattie took a deep breath as she moved the gear shift into Park. She sat at the end of her parents' driveway contemplating whether she had enough nerve to do this. After all, it had been a little over six years since she'd driven out of this driveway on her quest for freedom and adventure. It was peculiar how it seemed like it happened just yesterday, yet she felt decades older.

What would her father say when he opened the door and saw her standing there with the children? Would he have words of condemnation for her like when she'd left? As she now pondered his last words to her, she realized they'd been true. She hadn't been as mature as she'd thought she was at the time. She'd thought she'd known better than her parents. How wrong she'd been! Here, she was struggling after only five years of marriage, when her folks had been happily married for over twenty-five years. Perhaps they were a little wiser than what she'd given them credit for.

She looked into her rearview mirror at the children sleeping contently in their safety seats. Young Matthew was the spitting image of his father, while Lizzy favored her. She and Richard had definitely been blessed with beautiful, healthy children. Should she awaken them?

"*Hullo!*" a muffled male voice called out.

Mattie hardly noticed the Amish buggy pulling up beside her. The bearded man waved and she quickly rolled down her window.

"Mattie Riehl, is that you?"

Her mouth hung open. "Uh, Minister Fisher…Uncle Jonathan?" She forced a smile at one of her father's closest friends.

"Yep, it's me."

He glanced to the back of the car. "Are them your *kinner*?"

"Yes."

"Your folks will be pleased to see 'em." His broad smile caused lines to form around his large blue eyes. "Well, I was just heading up to your *dat's* place."

"Uh, Uncle Jonathan, will you please not say anything to my father? About me and the children, I mean."

Jonathan chuckled. "Well, I reckon I'd better just turn around and go back home then. 'Cuz there ain't no way I can keep Mattie Riehl's return to Paradise a secret."

"I don't know how long I'm staying yet."

"I see." He rubbed his beard. "How about if I just come back and see your *vatter* tomorrow?"

Mattie nodded. "Thank you, Jonathan."

"Be sure to stop by the house before you go back to the city. I'm certain sure your Aunt Susie will be wantin' to see ya. There are many things to catch up on. Did ya hear yet that Johnny and Judah got themselves hitched?"

Mattie thought of her fellow childhood rebel rousers with fondness. Oh, the mischief they'd gotten into! "No, I hadn't heard."

"I'm sure they'll be wantin' to see ya too and introduce you to their *fraas*. Hey, I've got an idea. Why don't we all get together for Christmas? That way, you'd be sure to see everybody."

This was all so overwhelming. She was unsure whether she'd even be welcomed back into her parents' home. How could she make plans for the next two weeks? "I don't know. Like I said, I'm not sure how long we'll stay."

Her uncle's countenance fell a bit, then he brightened suddenly. "You'll still be here. I'll pray for it. When will your husband be coming?"

A pang of regret shot through her heart. She hadn't even informed Richard of her whereabouts, not that he would care. Mattie frowned. "He's not."

"I see."

A deafening silence hung in the air for nearly a full minute, and Mattie knew she needed to move on before the tears began.

Finally, Jonathan smiled and tipped his hat. "Well, I reckon I'll let you go see your folks now."

As Mattie watched Jonathan's buggy disappear down the road, she heard soft noises from the back seat. She turned to look at the children, who had apparently awoken during her interchange with her uncle.

"Are you ready to go meet your grandpa and grandma?" She pasted on the most encouraging smile she could muster, despite the tumultuous uprising in the core of her being.

"I wanna go home." Mattie recognized the fear in her daughter's expression. It mirrored her own.

"We'll go home later. Don't you wanna meet Mommy's daddy and momma?" Mattie asked.

"Daddy?" Matthew perked up.

"You'll see Daddy later. He's still in the city." Did her two-year-old even understand her words?

She moved the gear shift back into the Drive position and slowly crept down the familiar lane she'd traveled many times. "See the big white house? That's where Mommy grew up."

"Swing!" Lizzy hollered.

"Wing?" Matthew repeated.

"Yes." Mattie smiled. "You may swing later. Right now, we're going to say hello to your grandparents."

Mattie quickly unfastened her seatbelt and climbed out of the driver's seat. It felt so good to stretch after a long drive. She unfastened the Matthew and Lizzy's child safety seats and allowed them to stretch as well before heading to the door.

As expected, four-year-old Lizzy bolted to the side yard and climbed up into the homemade wooden swing that hung from the largest Sycamore tree on the farm. It didn't matter that she'd never been to the property or didn't know the residents, all she knew was that she wanted to swing. *Oh, to be young and carefree again,* Mattie thought.

"Mommy and Matthew are going inside now. Do you want to stay out here by yourself, Lizzy?" Mattie's no-nonsense words caused her daughter to run back to the safety of her mother's side. "We can swing later," she assured the children.

"I want Daddy," Lizzy whined.

"Hush, now." Mattie quickly knocked on the front door and waited in trepidation. The sooner she got this greeting over with, the better. Maybe she should just turn around and go back home.

The door swung open and Mattie stood frozen.

THREE

Carson listened into his phone's earpiece.

Richard's voice sounded on the other end. "Carson, did Mattie say anything to Elisabeth? Did she tell her that she was leaving or anything?"

"No. That's why Elisabeth wanted me to call you. She's been trying to get a hold of Mattie."

"Well, I'm at the house and Mattie's not here. I've looked around. The house is completely silent."

"Did she leave a note or anything?"

"Not that I can see. I checked the table, the fridge, the bedroom... I don't know, Carson."

Carson detected concern in Richard's voice. "Where would she go?"

"I don't know. I called my mom and sister, and neither of them have heard from her. Elisabeth is the only other person I can think of who would know where she is. I guess it's possible that she's headed your way."

"Without calling? That's not like her." Carson sighed. He verbalized the thought that had been circling his mind. "Do you think she went back home?"

"You mean…to Paradise?"

"Yeah."

"No way. Mattie wouldn't go there. She said she'd never go back."

"She could have changed her mind."

"I don't think so." Richard was adamant.

"What are you going to do?"

Richard's heavy sigh came through the phone. "I don't know."

Carson paused a moment, contemplating whether or not to prod further. "Richard, what's going on with you and Mattie?"

"We're just going through a rough patch is all."

"A rough patch? Is that what you call it?" He didn't appreciate Richard's nonchalant assessment of the traumatic state of his marriage.

"What do you mean?"

"According to my wife, what you and Mattie are going through is more than just a rough patch. She told me that you and Mattie are considering divorce."

"Divorce? Mattie said that?"

"What do you expect when you're having an affair with another woman?"

"What the…? An affair? Is that what Mattie said?"

"She didn't have to."

"What do you mean?"

It was a good thing that they were just on the phone, because if Richard was standing before him in person, Carson was certain he'd have trouble controlling his fist. "You know what, this is really none of my business. But this affects *my* wife too and I don't appreciate it."

"Carson, I'm sorry."

"I'm not the one you should be apologizing to! Get your act together, Richard!" Carson couldn't help slamming the phone down. *Idiot!* It was hard to believe this was the man that led him to Christ a few years back.

God, please don't ever let me do anything like that to Elisabeth... And forgive me for my anger.

Her father stood before her in silence until her eyes met his. "Matilda?"

Mattie sighed. *I don't know if I can do this.*

She swallowed. "Hello, Dad." She managed an awkward smile.

"Come in." Mattie couldn't decipher her father's expression. Perhaps he was still in shock. After all, she'd had several hours to come to terms with the fact that she'd be seeing her father again. While her father, on the other hand, had been completely in the dark. She'd shown up on his doorstep unannounced, so he was entitled to some bewilderment.

She attempted to explain. "I was going to send a letter, but I didn't know if I could wait that long for a response."

Her father nodded and cleared his throat. "Maryanna," he called.

Tears rushed to Mattie's eyes as her mother walked into the room. Oh, how she'd missed her! Mattie immediately noticed more grey in her mother's hair. It seemed she'd aged more than Mattie had expected. Had stress from her leaving been the cause?

"Mattie?" Her mother rushed over and engulfed her in an immediate hug. "Oh, Mattie! I can't believe you're here!"

"I am." Mattie smiled. "And so are your grandchildren." She placed a hand on each of the children's heads, in turn. "This is Lizzy."

Lizzy smiled shyly. "I'm four and I like to swing."

Her mother chuckled.

Mattie continued, "And this…" – she looked up at her father and swallowed – "is Matthew."

"He's two," Lizzy added.

Her mother beckoned her father near and knelt down next to the children. "It's very nice to meet the two of you."

Young Matthew walked to his grandfather and held his arms out to him. Her father joyfully scooped his namesake into his arms and the gesture lifted Mattie's spirits. It seemed the children were making this transition a little easier for all of them, for which Mattie breathed a prayer of thanksgiving.

"Just two?" her father asked.

"Yes," Mattie confirmed. She understood her father's unspoken condemnation. Their Plain church didn't believe in artificial birth control. Of course, Mattie didn't either but she suspected her father thought she did. "For now."

Her father nodded, seemingly pleased. "And your husband? Where is he?"

"Daddy's still in the city," Lizzy volunteered.

"Hush now, Lizzy," Mattie reprimanded. "Richard's…uh… working."

"Daddy works a lot," Lizzy said.

"Liz-zy." Mattie warned.

"I see." Was her father suspicious? "Will he be coming later?"

"No. He won't be coming."

Her mother and father shared a look, then her mother spoke up. "How long will you and the children stay?"

"I don't know."

"Do you think you'll be here for Christmas?"

Mattie frowned. She and Richard hadn't once spent a Christmas apart since they'd met. What would he think if she didn't return home for the holidays? Would he even notice? "Maybe."

She wasn't sure if her father was pleased or disappointed. "And your husband approves of this?"

"Daddy don't live with us no more–"

"Lizzy!" Mattie scolded.

Lizzy's eyes welled up and she burst into tears. Mattie frowned and reached out to comfort her daughter, but Lizzy shunned her mother's outstretched arms and clung to her grand-mother instead.

Her father frowned. "Is *that* why you're here?"

"Richard does still live with us. He's just..." – she sighed – "...he's not always home." She eyed both of her parents. "I'd rather not discuss this in front of the children."

She didn't miss her father's pointed gaze. "Does he *know* you're here?"

"No," she whispered.

"Maryanna, why don't you take the children outside to play on the swing?" her father suggested.

"Swing!" Lizzy brightened again.

Her mother offered a sympathetic smile. Maryanna took young Matthew from her husband and led the children out the back door.

Her father turned back to her. "Matilda, if you expect to stay here, you need to be honest with your mother and me. What's going on? Are you in trouble?"

Mattie's hands became clammy. "No. I mean, yes, but I don't know if it's the kind you're thinking."

"Just speak to me straight, Matilda. Why aren't you with your husband? Or why isn't he here with you?"

Did they really need to discuss this now? Couldn't it wait until tomorrow...or next week? "Richard's seeing another wom-an." Tears surfaced at her words. "I don't think he cares that I'm not at home. *If* he's even noticed yet. "

"I see." Her father remained silent for what seemed like a fortnight. "Then you may stay for as long as necessary." He stood up, walked over to her, and offered an awkward hug. "I'm sorry, *dochder*."

At his words, the floodgates opened and she was no longer able to contain her grief. She wept in her father's arms for as long as she needed to. "I'm sorry too."

After six long years of contention, she and her father were finally on the path to healing. And although the road was painful, it felt good.

FOUR

Carson sidled up to Elisabeth and playfully bumped her hip. "Finished with your Christmas shopping?"

She met his eyes with curiosity and grinned. "Yes. And you?"

"Yesterday." Carson smiled. "That means you're free this evening then?"

"What do you have in mind?"

His eyes sparkled. "A sleigh ride."

"A sleigh ride? But the children already had their baths."

"Which is perfect. Jacob and Rachel can put them to bed after supper."

"Jacob and Rachel? You mean you want just *us* to go on a sleigh ride?"

"Why not? It'll be fun with just the two of us." He nuzzled her neck. "And romantic."

"Romantic? What are you up to?"

"Me? I just want to spend an evening alone with my wife. This is completely innocent, I promise."

"Mm hm. And where do you plan to get the sleigh?"

"We can borrow one from the Glicks, or the Fishers."

"But you don't know how to drive a sleigh."

Carson frowned. "You don't want to go, do you?"

"Of course, I do."

"Good, because I thought you might want to stop by and see the Beilers' new little one."

"Oh, that's right! Luke and Brianna just had their baby." She smiled. What a blessing new life brought! "We've been so busy, I nearly forgot."

"Now you can give them the blanket you've been crocheting," he reminded.

She nodded. "I'm glad I finally finished it." She'd always loved crocheting; it brought a deep sense of satisfaction each time a project was completed. *Idle hands are the devils tools.* How many times had she heard that saying repeated, while growing up in her Amish community? But she knew that hands need not be idle to do the devil's bidding; for it could be accomplished just the same with busy hands, with feet running to mischief, and oftentimes with a loose tongue.

"Why don't you get ready? They should be here any time."

Elisabeth tiptoed and kissed his cheek. "Yes, my love." She quickly disappeared into the bedroom to prepare for an evening with her thoughtful husband.

"What are we doing at my folks' place?"

Carson reached over and squeezed Elisabeth's hand. "You left your ice skates here the last time we visited, remember?"

"Ice skates? I thought we were going sledding."

"We are. But don't you want to get your ice skates, so you'll have them when you need them?"

Elisabeth shrugged. "I guess." Her eyes shot to the vehicle's dash clock. "Do we have time right now?"

"Sure. We don't have to stay long."

"You *know* my parents. They'll want us to stay and talk."

"We can remind them that we're on a date and that the children are at home with Jacob and Rachel."

"Okay."

Carson's brow shot up. "If I didn't know any better, I'd think you're trying to avoid your parents."

"Me? Of course, not. It's just, you know how much I worry when we're away from the *kinner*."

"*Kinner*?" An amused expression briefly danced across his face.

"Children," she corrected.

Carson chuckled. "Lincoln said something the other day with a Pennsylvania Dutch accent."

"*Ach*, do you think he got it from me? I'd hoped I'd lost my accent." She frowned.

"Why do you say that? It's only natural to revert back to it now and again. I think it's cute."

"Cute?"

"And it's part of your cultural heritage. You shouldn't be ashamed to be yourself." He reached for her hand. "I love you just the way you are – adorable accent and all."

Elisabeth's lip jutted out a bit. "I just thought that I'd lost it, that's all."

"I think your return to Amish Country and being away from the city has caused you to pick it up again. When we met, I didn't even notice an accent. Or if I did, it was slight." Carson glanced at Elisabeth and frowned. "You're happy living near your parents' place, aren't you?"

"Of course. I love where we live. I wouldn't want to live anywhere else. It's perfect – just an hour away from my folks, yet close enough to the city so you can check with your clients once a week."

Carson picked up Elisabeth's hand and grazed it with his lips. "Good, because I want my wife to be happy."

Elisabeth's head snapped backward. "Was that Luke and Brianna's buggy we just passed?"

Carson shrugged and chuckled. "I can't decipher whose buggy is whose. I believe that is a gift only the Amish possess. They all look the same to me. A buggy's a buggy."

"If you're around them all your life, it's easy to tell whose is whose. They're usually distinct in one way or another. My folks' buggy, for example, has four rectangular reflectors that go straight across the back. The Fishers' buggy has three on each side. The Brennemans' buggy has differently shaped reflectors and there's two on each side toward the bottom and one near the top in the middle."

"I guess I never really took those kinds of things into consideration." He lightly rubbed the stubble on his chin.

"And then, the horses are different too. Not only by what breed they are, but also in the way they trot. A person can usually tell who it is by just listening. Take *Mamm* and *Dat's* driving horse, Peanut. He has a smooth steady gait, unlike my brother's mare that thinks she's still on the race track."

"I thought that depended on who's holding the reins."

"That does have something to do with it, but not always. Horses tend to have a mind of their own sometimes."

"This city boy wouldn't know."

"Former city boy," she reminded him.

Carson smiled as they pulled into the Schrocks' familiar driveway. "Let's go say hello to your parents."

Elisabeth sipped on the hot apple cider her mother handed her just a few minutes earlier. She looked at the familiar surroundings. It occurred to her that no matter how far she traveled, her folks' place always felt like home. She briefly wondered how many children grew up with that kind of security, knowing home would be the same place they grew up and the place where their folks would live out their days on earth. She'd truly had a goodly heritage.

"Was that Luke and Brianna's buggy I saw on the road?" Elisabeth leaned back in the hickory rocker, another comfort from childhood. She momentarily pondered the possibility of securing a couple of the chairs for her own home.

"*Jah*. Luke stopped by to say hello. He didn't want to stay long because Brianna's at home with their new *boppli*." Her mother's face beamed.

"Have you seen the baby yet?"

"Oh, yes." Her mother nodded. "I stayed with Brianna for a couple of days after the *boppli* was born. He's a strong, handsome little guy, like his *dat*."

Elisabeth glanced over at Carson and her father, who seemed to be lost in their own conversation. He caught her eye and winked.

"Really? How often do you see them?"

"They come by nearly once a week. You know, I kind of feel like *Der Herr* gave your *vatter* and me a new *dochder* when Brianna moved to Paradise. I think she sees us as her folks too, although she's got *Englisch* kin in New York."

A small pang of jealousy crept into Elisabeth's heart, but she mentally rebuked it. "Brianna's a nice girl."

"*Jah*. And she and Luke make a perfect couple. More so than you and Luke did, I think."

"Well, I guess God knew what He was doing."

"That, He did."

"*Mamm*, I've always wondered something." Elisabeth locked eyes with her mother.

"*Jah?*"

"Well, did you *really* think that Brianna was me? I mean, I know we could've passed for identical twins, but…I don't know, we just seem so different to me."

"Honestly, I had some doubts. I think we all did. But you had been gone to the city for two years. People can change a lot during that time. Especially when becoming *Englisch*. And if you *had* been in an accident and didn't remember who you were or anything about your past…"

"I guess I can see that. But what about my accent? Brianna's speech is much more *Englisch*."

"Sometimes people pick up other accents easily and you hadn't been back home or around other Amish." She smiled thoughtfully. "Part of it could have been that we wanted you home so badly that we didn't even think twice about it *not* being you. We just figured that because you'd been *Englisch* and because of the accident that you were different now."

"Well, I admit that I was a little jealous. Here, I come home and someone else had taken over the life I had. She won her way into your hearts and Luke even married her! Let's just say that it was a bit of a shock to me." Elisabeth frowned.

"I can see that. And we were shocked, too, when we heard that you came back and that Brianna was somebody else." *Mamm* reached over and touched Elisabeth's hand. "We loved her then like she was you, like one of our own. And we still do. But that doesn't mean that we love you any less. We're just thankful to *Der Herr* that we've been blessed with both of you."

Elisabeth nodded and Carson caught her eye.

Carson stood up. "Well, Ben, Leah, it's been nice talking with you, but your daughter and I have to go. We're supposed to be on a date and we still have to stop by the Beilers' before our sleigh ride."

Dat stood up. "It was *gut* seeing you two again. And we'll be seeing you again on Christmas, right?"

Carson looked to Elisabeth and she nodded.

"Did you get your skates, Lis?"

"Yep."

Mamm spoke up, "Oh, I almost forgot to ask. Have you seen Mattie Riehl since she's been in town?"

Elisabeth turned back to face her mother. "Mattie's here?"

"Heard she and the *kinner* arrived at her folks place a couple of days ago."

Elisabeth stared at Carson with her mouth agape. "That's where she went!"

If Mattie returned home, wouldn't that mean that she and her father had finally reconciled? Imagine that! Elisabeth never thought she'd live to see that day. Could it be true?

Well, there was only one way to find out.

"Carson, let's go now?"

Her husband nodded.

She eyed her mother again. "By the way, *Mamm*, it's Mattie Greene."

30

Her mother smiled. "That's right. I couldn't remember her husband's name."

"Thanks for telling me about Mattie, *Mamm*. She and I have some catching up to do."

FIVE

*B*rianna hesitantly approached Carson when Elisabeth disappeared into the kitchen. Since her accident nearly five years ago, she'd had little contact with her former beau, and they'd never really engaged in conversation outside a group setting. But recently, she'd been having more and more questions about the past – questions only Carson would have the answers to.

She stared at her hands as they twisted in her lap. "I, uh, have been remembering more."

Carson eyed his ex-girlfriend. "That's great."

She attempted to fake a smile. "Uh, yeah, well. It was about *our* past. About you and me."

"What did you remember?" Carson briefly wondered if it might be better for Brianna *not* to remember some things. But their past was what it was, and there was no going back and changing it. Fortunately, God was good and he offered forgiveness when we've made messes of our lives. However, the consequences of sin don't die.

"Did we visit some tropical place? I remembered being on a large fancy boat with you."

"That would've been our cruise to Mexico celebrating our first anniversary as a couple."

"And we…" Brianna's cheeks flamed, but she continued on. "We shared a room, didn't we?"

That would've been one of the things he wished she didn't remember. He nodded.

Brianna swallowed. "I'd kinda hoped that I'd been pure before Luke and I married."

That, she was not. "I'm sorry."

"Was that the only time?"

"I'm afraid not. It was one of many, unfortunately."

"Oh." She rubbed her head and frowned. "Carson, what kind of a person was I? I mean, am I all that different now?"

"You're very different now. And so am I." Carson paused a moment to gather his thoughts. "I think God has worked a miracle in both of our lives. And He used your accident to do that."

"So, you got saved after my accident too?"

"No, I'd been saved for about two years before the accident. I'd tried to talk to you about it many times, but you had absolutely no interest in the things of God."

"Really?"

"Yeah, really. I've wondered many times if God let things happen the way they did to get us to where we are today. It's been a pretty crazy ride, huh?"

"Definitely crazy." Brianna sighed. "Where do you think we'd be if the accident hadn't happened?"

"That's hard to tell."

"Do you think *we* would have married?"

He shrugged. "Don't know. I'd wanted to marry you, but the more you rejected God, the more distant our relationship became. I knew I could never marry you if you didn't accept Christ. My pastor said that was a recipe for failure. Precious few marriages last when a couple is unequally yoked."

"I'm glad the accident happened, then. Despite all the heartache it brought, I think there was more good."

"So, what did your family think about you marrying an Amish man?"

Brianna laughed. "They were surprised for sure and for certain. They said that I could probably get an annulment on the grounds of mental instability. Of course, I refused their suggestion. Why would I want to leave Luke? He's the best thing that ever happened to me. We love each other and I can't imagine my life without him." She shook her head. "They told me that I would come to regret it – especially when I remembered who I was. But I've never regretted it, not even for a second. How could I? I think I have a wonderful life. This is the life I know and love."

"Well, I admit. Never in a million years would I have *ever* pictured you becoming Amish. It's pretty much the exact opposite of how you used to be."

"How was I?"

"Well, you were definitely concerned with fashion trends. You insisted on wearing the newest and best clothes available. If your parents weren't wealthy, you would have been in a heap of debt. You were pretty feministic too, I'd say. There's no way you would have let a man be the head of the house. And you were independent. Not to mention, you hated long dresses. Yeah, so pretty much completely opposite."

"Did you ever think *you* would marry someone who used to be Amish?"

Carson chuckled. "Can't say I did. Before your accident, I thought we'd eventually get married. I thought that somehow I'd convince you to become a Christian."

"What did you think when you thought that I'd died?"

"It tore me up." Carson's hand balled into a fist as he remembered that day. "I was so concerned with your eternal destination, and I was upset that you wouldn't even listen to me. I thought that God had given you one last chance to hear the truth and you refused. I was so mad at you for your stubbornness. And at the devil. I thought that surely you'd gone to hell."

"That's a scary thought."

He nodded once. "I guess God knew all along that you would eventually turn to Him, so He gave you another chance."

"I'm so glad He did." Brianna smiled. "And, Carson. Thank you for trying to tell me about God. I know I didn't appreciate it at the time, but I can't help but think that somewhere in my subconscious mind, I wanted to know. Maybe that was a stepping stone, though neither of us realized it then."

"In that case, I guess it was worth my frustration. We just never know what God might be doing inside a person's heart."

Carson looked up and noticed his wife standing in the doorway. "Elisabeth." He smiled. "How long have you been standing there?"

"A little while." Her smile seemed forced. "I didn't want to interrupt your conversation."

"Oh, I hear the baby." Brianna abruptly stood up. "She's probably in need of a change and starving. Or thinks she is."

Carson and Elisabeth watched her flee the room in haste.

"Wow! She doesn't mess around." Carson chuckled.

Elisabeth frowned.

"What's wrong?" He reached for her hand, but she shook her head in refusal. "Talk to me, Lis."

Tears sprung to her eyes. "Do you wish you'd married her?"

"*What*?"

"If she'd gotten saved." She sighed heavily, and struggled to hold back tears. "You wanted to marry her, right?"

Carson raked a hand through his hair. "Whoa, whoa, whoa! Where'd all this come from?"

"You just said–"

"No."

"No?"

"No. I don't wish I'd married her. I'm in love with *you*. It does no good to dig up the past and ponder what might have been. God knew exactly what we both needed." He smiled and drew her close. "Each other."

"But Mattie and Richard—"

"*We're* not Mattie and Richard. I already told you, babe. You're stuck with me." He bent down and pressed his lips to hers. "If you want to get rid of me, you'll have to kill me off."

Elisabeth giggled.

"I'm totally serious."

She sobered. "What do you think will happen with Mattie and Richard?"

"I really don't know. Hopefully, Richard will wake up and realize what he's doing."

She looked toward the bedroom and smiled when she heard the newborn cry. Little ones were so special. "I want to see Mattie tomorrow."

"I think that's a good idea. I wonder if Richard knows where she is yet."

Elisabeth shrugged. "Maybe we should let Mattie call him."

"And if she doesn't?" He eyed his wife. "A man should know where his family is, even if they're at odds. If you couldn't get a hold of Mattie, I'm guessing Richard can't either."

"That's not a word." Jacob Schrock eyed his beautiful wife from across the Scrabble board.

"It is too!" Rachel protested.

"Shh...you're gonna wake up the *kinner*." Jacob glanced at the clock on the wall and wondered when Carson and Elisabeth would return. "Just because *you* use a word all the time doesn't mean it's acceptable in a Scrabble game. 'Thingamajig' is not a word. Look it up in the dictionary."

"You used '*ferhoodled*'! That's not in the dictionary either."

"But it's an Amish word. We agreed that Amish words were acceptable, remember?"

"That's not fair."

Jacob reached over the table and grasped Rachel's hand.

"Stop it." She pulled her hand back. "I don't want to hold your hand right now. I'm mad at you."

"You can keep the word, *schatzi*." He forced the lower corner of his lip not to rise, although difficult. A small thrill tickled his soul whenever he innocently offended his wife. Perhaps it was because she made a certain expression he couldn't resist? Or was it the fact that they would kiss and make up later?

"No. I'm not a cheater."

"Í didn't say you were a cheater."

"You may as well have." She planted a hand on her hip.

"Honey, I only said that 'thingamajig' is not a word. I made no reference to cheating."

"If I keep the word and win the game, you'll say I didn't win fair and square. If I don't keep it, I'll give up all those points. Either way, I lose."

"*Ach*, Rachel." Jacob looked up toward the ceiling and raised his hands. "God, why did you have to make women so difficult?"

"I'm not difficult."

"No, not you. Never. Did I say difficult? I meant delightful."
He smiled and rose from the table.

"Where are you going?"

He took her hand and kissed it. "Let's put the game away
and call it a tie." He tugged at the hand he'd just kissed. "Come,
schatzi, let's go snuggle on the couch."

"Oo…snuggling on the couch. Now that sounds like a good
idea." A male voice resounded. Carson's voice. "What do you
say, Elisabeth?"

Jacob chuckled. "Carson, you're back!"

"I'm afraid you two will have to go home and snuggle on
your own couch." Carson smiled. "How were the children?"

"They were great." Rachel smiled, then proceeded to put the
Scrabble tiles away. "I think they missed our *kinner*, though."

"It would've been too late for them. That's why we left them
at your folks' place," Jacob reminded his wife.

Carson nodded. "How are Saul and Chloe doing these
days?"

Rachel smiled. "They're good. They love having the *kin-skinner* over."

"And they're spending the night." Jacob smiled and raised
his eyebrows twice in quick succession.

"Thanks for watching the children, but I think it's time for
you two lovebirds to scoot." Carson winked at Elisabeth.

"You're right. Ready, Rach?" Jacob tilted his head.

"*Jah*. Did you turn the buggy heater on already?"

He rubbed his hands together. "About ten minutes ago. It should be nice and toasty."

"You should have a pleasant drive. There isn't much traffic on the road tonight," Elisabeth interjected.

"Are you sure you don't want to leave the buggy here and pick it up tomorrow? It's quite a long drive. I could give you a ride," Carson offered.

"Nah. I like it. It reminds me of our courtin' days." Jacob pulled his wife to his side, then he waved to Elisabeth. "Good-night, sis."

"Thanks again," Carson said as Jacob and Rachel stepped out the door.

SIX

$\mathcal{R}$ichard closed the door behind him and walked into his house.

Silence smacked him in the face.

There was nothing. No one. No Mattie. No Lizzy. No Matthew. Just himself and the deafening silence.

He hadn't felt this alone in years. Even when Mattie was angry with him and no longer greeted him at the door when he returned home, there was still noise. Quiet humming, footsteps, the children playing, something. But never dead silence.

Richard walked through the living room, past the dining room and the kitchen. He paused only when he reached the entrance to his and Mattie's bedroom. The door was open, just how he'd left it when he came home to search for his wife a couple days ago.

He didn't want to go inside but he took a step anyway. Memories immediately assaulted him. Memories of shared love, shared arguments, shared tears. At the moment, he didn't wish to relive any of them. But they came anyway, flitted through his mind and heart and then vanished, leaving him with only a hollow ache inside.

Richard sat on the bed, then slid down to the floor.

"Oh, God," he moaned. "How have we fallen this far?"

Of course, he was answered with silence. But he already knew the answer to his question. Carson had voiced it for him not more than an hour ago.

"We found her, Richard."

Richard sighed into the cell phone. "Where is she?"

"She went home."

"To her parents' place?"

"Yes. Elisabeth and I are going to visit her tomorrow."

"Thanks for telling me, Carson."

"What are you going to do?"

"What do you mean?"

"What do I mean? This is your wife, *Richard! Remember? The one you vowed to love? The one you vowed to honor and cherish? What are you going to do to fix this mess you've made?" Frustration was clear in his friend's voice.*

It wouldn't do any good to deny his friend's cutting words. "I don't know."

"Well, you'd better figure it out fast, unless you plan on filing divorce papers."

Frustration began to mount. "This really isn't any of your business, Carson."

"You're right. It isn't my business. But it is God's. You and Mattie both stood at that altar and pledged your lives to each

other in God's holy name. And now you're not giving Him the time of day."

Richard didn't know what to say. His excuses seemed so inadequate when faced with the truth of his circumstances.

A sigh came from the other end. Then silence. Finally, Carson said, "When was the last time you read your Bible, Richard?"

"I-"

"No. Don't answer to me. I don't have anything to do with it. It's between you and God, Richard. You answer to Him."

Carson hung up.

Richard knew his friend had been right in at least one regard. He had to do *something*. He just wasn't sure what to do *now*.

Mattie's gaze focused on an approaching vehicle when she heard the crunch of snow under its tires. Carson and Elisabeth barreled up the lane with their children. Apparently, they'd discovered where she was.

She abruptly stopped the swing and turned to her daughter. "Do you want to play with Lincoln and Jacob?"

Lizzy squealed and rushed for the car, her answer apparent.

Mattie couldn't help a grin tugging at the corner of her mouth at her daughter's enthusiasm, and she allowed the expression to take over her face as she followed Lizzy.

The little ones rushed off to the swing with Lizzy in the lead just as Mattie reached the Volvo. Carson smiled and offered a side hug. "Good to see you, Mattie." He pointed toward the children. "I'd better go make sure they don't get into too much trouble."

"Hello, Carson," Mattie smiled as she watched her friend's husband meander toward the playground. The comfort of seeing good familiar friends warmed her aching heart just a bit. Elisabeth squeezed Mattie into an embrace and she shut her eyes against the tears threatening to surface.

"It's so wonderful to see you, Mattie."

"You too, Lis," she released the difficult words into her friend's freshly shampooed tresses.

Elisabeth pulled away. "It seems like forever since we last talked."

Mattie nodded and inclined her head toward the house. "Would you like to come inside?"

"Sure. I haven't seen your parents in a while. It'll be nice to see them again"

"Well, Dad isn't home right now, but Mom is. She'll be happy to see you."

Her mother opened the door just as they reached it. "Oh, Elisabeth, I haven't seen you in ages! How are you?"

"Good. It's nice to see you, Maryanna," Elisabeth replied with a hug. "Carson and I are doing wonderful and the *kinner* are growing like weeds," she said, slipping back into her native tongue.

"They always do when they're young. How many do you have now?"

"Just four."

"Well, I'm sure that number won't remain for very long." Mattie's mother laughed.

"I hope not." Elisabeth grinned, her cheeks pinkened slightly.

"Well, I'll leave you two alone so you can catch up. I'll just be in the kitchen making hot cocoa for everyone. As soon as it's ready, I'll call you two down." She turned to her daughter. "Oh, and Mattie, little Matthew is upstairs sleeping in his and Lizzy's room. Just so you know."

"Thanks, Mom." Mattie gave her mother a kiss before starting for the upstairs. She gestured toward her bedroom, inviting her best friend inside.

"Wow, this is just how I remember it!" Elisabeth surveyed the room and turned to Mattie. "Is it difficult being back in this same room?"

Mattie shrugged. "Somewhat. Brings back memories. I was so foolish, ready to leave all of this behind and jump into the unknown *Englisch* world."

Elisabeth laughed. "I remember. That was *all* you talked about at the time. New York City. And it wasn't long until *I* was hot on your trail, so full of my own rebellious ways. I can't say that was the wisest thing I've ever done."

Mattie nodded.

"But I must admit, it sure did end up well. If I hadn't jumped the fence, none of these amazing blessings would have been mine – Carson, the *kinner*. God had me in the palm of His hand all along."

"I wish I could say the same," Mattie murmured.

Elisabeth sighed and plopped down next to her friend on the bed. She squeezed her hand. "Your life *still* abounds with blessings, Mattie Greene. You have a roof over your head, a family to take care of you, a great friend to talk to," she laughed, "two children who love you, and most importantly, a God Who will never leave you." A twinkle lit her eye. "And once God whacks your husband upside the head so he comes to his senses, you'll have him again too."

Mattie couldn't help a little chuckle. "Oh, Lis."

"What? I'm serious." She grinned.

They laughed for a moment, and then Mattie's laughter turned to tears. Elisabeth's arms wrapped around her friend as she sobbed.

If only things were different.

Elisabeth felt like throttling Richard for wounding Mattie so. But she did her best to control her anger. It wasn't going to help anything, and since Richard wasn't here to offer himself up as a punching bag, she returned to the task at hand – comforting her best friend.

"Just let it all out," she murmured into Mattie's hair, rubbing circles on her back.

Finally, Mattie calmed herself and sat up, her eyes reddened and watery. Elisabeth offered a tissue and she blew long and hard.

"I don't know what I'm gonna do, Lis." Mattie wiped away another tear that trailed her cheek. "I can't raise these children alone. They need their father."

"You won't be alone. You have a lot of people who will help you, Mattie."

"Did you know that children of divorced parents live five years less on average than children from intact families?" More tears escaped her eyelashes. "I don't want to give them an early death sentence!"

Mattie always had been overly dramatic, but Elisabeth certainly felt her concerns. "Their time is in *Der Herr's* hands."

"And I'm pregnant again," she blurted out.

The thought brought a measure of comfort to Elisabeth. If Mattie and Richard still had intimate moments together, there was hope that their marriage wasn't as bad off as she'd thought.

"Richard said he only wanted two."

Elisabeth smiled slightly. "I think God's plans supersede Richard's, don't you?"

Mattie shrugged.

"Do you think he'll be upset?" Lis frowned.

"I don't know."

Elisabeth smiled and raised a brow. "Mattie, I thought you and Richard hadn't had any...uh... contact lately."

Mattie blushed slightly. "Well, we have had *some* off and on. I'm about eight weeks along, so..."

"How long have you known?"

"Three weeks."

"And you haven't said anything till now? Why didn't you call me?"

"You've been busy." Mattie frowned.

"Always. But never too busy for things that really matter. You know you can crash on me any time."

A corner of Mattie's mouth lifted a bit. "I know. You've always been there for me."

"I wouldn't say that. God's the one Who's always been there for you."

Mattie looked away.

"What is it?"

Mattie scowled. "God could have prevented all this."

Elisabeth sighed. She'd prayed Mattie wouldn't turn away from God when she needed Him most. The root of bitterness was like an all-consuming disease. "Perhaps."

"It's true, Lis. He could have prevented all this, but He didn't. Why?"

"People still make their own choices, Mattie. God won't force people to do the right thing, or keep them from sinning. He gives each person a choice, their own free will."

"Why hasn't He answered my prayers? Instead of Richard and me making up, he moves in with his secretary! I honestly think that God doesn't care about me or the children."

"You know that's not true."

"No, I don't. If God cares, why is He letting Richard ruin our family? Why is He ignoring my pleas?"

"I don't know all the reasons, but I do know that God is good and He can be trusted. If you and Richard belong to Him, He *will* work this out for good."

"It's so hard to trust Him when all I see is darkness around me."

"Take His hand and let Him lead you out, Mattie. Cast your cares upon him. Give Him your yoke, He will carry it for you."

"I don't know if I can."

"It's the only way to find peace. The Bible says that the king's heart is in the hand of the Lord. If God can change a king's heart, I know He can change Richard's too. You can't give up." Elisabeth rubbed Mattie's shoulder. "Mattie, may I pray with you?"

Mattie shrugged. "Sure."

Both bowed their heads and Elisabeth poured her heart out to God, asking Him to intercede on Mattie's behalf. They embraced briefly before Maryanna called them down for hot cocoa.

"Thank you, Lis." Mattie wiped away another tear. "I'm blessed to have you as a friend."

"As am I." Elisabeth smiled. "Come on. Let's go join the children for some hot chocolate. Chocolate always makes everything better." She winked.

SEVEN

Pennsylvania? She had gone to Pennsylvania...*back to her parents? Mattie said she'd never go back. Apparently, she changed her mind*, Richard's thoughts discouraged him. *If she would rather face her parents than work this out, we're definitely in trouble.*

She suspects I'm having an affair? And told Elisabeth we're considering getting a divorce?

He sighed. It didn't make any sense. There had to be something he was missing.

Richard made his way to the bedroom – the one he hadn't slept in in weeks – and searched for Mattie's box of letters. Surely her parents' address had to be nestled in the bountiful stack of floral stationary. Most of the letters were from Elisabeth or various relatives in Pennsylvania.

An unaddressed envelope caught his eye. Only one word was written on the outside. *Mattie.* The handwriting appeared to be derived from a masculine source, judging by the simplicity. It wasn't her father's handwriting. Curiosity got the best of him and he quickly pulled the letter out. *Hey, Mattie. I miss the fun times we had together. If you ever return to visit your folks, be sure to come by my place so we can catch up. Johnny*

Richard stared at the brief letter in his hand. Who was it from? Was this Johnny guy a former love interest? And when did Mattie receive this? Had she been corresponding with the note's writer and, if so, for how long? Dread threatened to consume his thoughts. He quickly placed the letter aside and continued his original search.

There it was. He recognized this letter from years ago, when he'd encouraged Mattie to make amends with her father. She'd refused, and Richard now wondered if Mattie harbored bitterness in her heart. Perhaps that had been the root of *their* troubles. Had Mattie let her bitterness for her father turn into anger towards *him*?

He jotted the address down so he could enter it into his GPS later.

Richard glanced to the backseat of his vehicle and briefly smiled. He thought he'd done a pretty good job this year picking out special gifts for Mattie and the children, although his gift-wrapping skills definitely needed some work. A professional gift-wrapper he was not. He grimaced when he noticed that one of the crudely wrapped gifts had an open spot, revealing its contents. How did he miss that? He certainly didn't possess the same domestic skills as his wife did, and probably never would. *Oh, well. It was the thought that counted, right?*

His eyes moved to the special card on top of the stack. Would Mattie accept his gift to her? It seemed like lately she wouldn't even give him the time of day, let alone carry on a meaningful conversation with him. How on earth had their relationship come to such a broken state?

He realized he hadn't done everything right. He could have listened to Mattie more and worked a little less. He should have provided more for her emotional needs. And her wants. Mattie seemed to have a lot of wants. Not that he blamed her.

She'd grown up in a small Mennonite/Amish community, and that meant she'd been sheltered. She'd been brave coming to the Big Apple all alone at the age of eighteen. She was so young and innocent and really had no clue about the real world. She'd discovered that pretty quickly upon her arrival. How would she have fared if they hadn't met that fateful day, when she'd been drug into the alley by that ruthless attacker? If he hadn't been there to rescue her, would she have stayed in the city or gone back home? Would she still be alive even? He cringed at the thought. Thank God He'd put him in the right place at the right time. Richard briefly closed his eyes and gave thanks for protecting Mattie that day. There was no doubt God had been guiding his steps.

But where was God *now*? It seemed their most forceful attack from the enemy had gone unnoticed. If God didn't help them out of this potential catastrophe, there was no doubt in

Richard's mind that their ship would sink. And that was simply unacceptable. He refused to allow this marriage to fail.

Being away from his family had been excruciating. He *had to* find a way to get back into Mattie's heart.

Hopefully, his gift to her would do the trick.

EIGHT

*M*attie turned to look at her phone when it rang. *Richard.* Again.

She ignored it and sighed. She'd had enough of his lies and excuses. If he sincerely wanted to talk, he'd come find her. She seriously doubted he would, and she smothered the flicker of hope that he would come to her and plead for forgiveness. And even if he did, would she grant it? Mattie wasn't sure anymore. She would love to be back to how she and Richard were, young and in love without all the complications. But she didn't see how they could ever return to that bliss, not with Richard's unfaithfulness. How was she supposed to trust him now?

Mattie shoved down the lump that fought for possession of her throat. She'd cried enough lately to fill an Olympic-sized pool. She was tired of it.

Her phone rang again and she groaned. When would Richard get that she didn't want to talk to him? She was almost tempted to answer it just so she could give him a piece of her mind.

She glanced at it and frowned. It was a number she didn't recognize. She picked it up. "Hello?"

"Is... Is this Mattie Riehl?" It sounded like an Amish man. His voice niggled at her memory. No, surely it couldn't be.

She didn't correct him. "Yes, it is. Who is this?"

"'Tis Johnny Fisher, your cousin."

She gasped. "It *is* you! I thought it sounded like your voice. How are you doing, Johnny? It's great to hear from you after all this time."

"*Jah*, it has been a long time. I am doing *gut*. *Dat* told me you had come back and I was wonderin' if you'd like to meet and talk."

"Yes, of course. I would love to. When?"

"I was thinkin' breakfast tomorrow at seven."

"All right. And where do you want to meet?"

"I was thinkin' we could go to the Cracker Barrel in Lancaster."

"That sounds great. I can't wait to see you, Johnny."

"*Jah*, I'm certain sure there will be much for us to catch up on. I'll see you then."

"Okay, see you."

"Goodbye." Her cousin hung up.

"Wow," Mattie said to herself. He sounded just like he did six years ago.

Mattie smiled at her cousin across the table. "It's really great to see you, Johnny. It's been such a long time since we've talked."

"*Jah.* 'Bout six years, I'm thinkin'."

She nodded.

"What's happened while I've been gone? I thought I heard a little rumor that you and Judah went and got yourselves hitched."

Johnny nodded, a grin spreading across his face. "Yep. Judah married Sarah Anne Yoder and I got hitched to sweet little Ellie Weaver."

Mattie's jaw dropped. "Sarah Anne? Ellie?" She started laughing. "I thought Sarah Anne despised Judah! And Ellie, she's so shy, how'd you ever get her to ride home with you?"

Her cousin chuckled at her reaction. "That's about what everybody said. Turns out Sarah Anne didn't mind Judah so much when he wasn't acting like a hooligan. She's been shapin' him up right good, though he's still ornery as ever. Just hides it better now. They've already got two little ones, Elias and Jonathan."

"Wow. I can hardly believe it. What about you and Ellie?"

His eyes twinkled mischievously. "Well, that one's a different story. You see, I was plannin' on going home from a Singin' with Lyddie Brenneman, but she went with Isaac Miller instead."

"He's Daniel and Abigail's son, right?"

"*Jah*, their oldest. Anyway, I hadn't rode home once by myself from a Singing and I didn't like the thought of starting to, so I figured I'd ask someone else. Most of 'em already had rides

59

so I found myself walkin' up to Ellie. I'd never even thought much about her, probably because she was so quiet. But I went up and asked her if I could take her home in my buggy."

"What'd she say?"

"No."

Mattie giggled. "She actually turned you down?"

He nodded. "Yep. I wasn't really sure what to say 'cuz I didn't expect her to have the courage to refuse, but she did. I thought about it for a while after that and when the next Singin' came along, I asked her again."

"Couldn't take no for an answer?"

"You know me." He grinned. "Of course not. Finally, I got it out of her why she always said no. She had promised to herself and *Gott* that she wouldn't kiss no one till she married and she knew for sure and for certain that I wouldn't want to wait."

"Wow. That's a great idea. So how'd you two ever end up married?"

"Just wait, you'll see.

"Her promise intrigued me and, after asking her about two months straight, she finally said yes, as long as I didn't try to touch her and took her directly home. I agreed and that was our first buggy ride."

"And you guys didn't kiss until your wedding day? Wow."

"Oh no, I kissed her before that." Pride swallowed his voice.

"You did?"

A smirk tugged at Johnny's mouth. "I kissed her on her cheek, forehead, and one time even her nose."

Mattie smiled. "Her nose?"

"I was aimin' for her mouth but she dodged and then threatened to walk home if I didn't behave."

Mattie laughed. "Sounds like you married the right person."

He nodded, face bright with happiness. "I did. And now we have two *kinner*, Noah and Lavina, and another one on the way."

"Congratulations, Johnny. I'd love to meet them all some time."

"We're having a Christmas gathering at *Daed*'s on the twenty-fourth. You're welcome to come and meet everyone there."

Mattie smiled. "I think I'd like that."

Johnny took a gulp of his coffee before turning back to her. "And what about you? What's happened since you jumped the fence?"

Mattie sighed, though she knew he was bound to ask. If only she had a satisfying answer. "Well, shortly after I moved to New York City, I met a man named Richard. He rescued me, actually. Some vile man was pulling me down an alley and he came and took care of him. Very brave," she murmured wistfully.

"Love at first sight?" Her cousin gave her a wink.

The corners of her mouth curved upward a tad. "Not quite, though it wasn't far behind.

"Through a series of events, we began dating and eventually married. After about a year, we had our first child, Elisabeth."

"Ah. Named for your friend Elisabeth Schrock."

"Elisabeth Welch now, but yes, Lizzy was named after her. She was a beautiful baby and though she took her time coming, she was very much worth it. She's four now and introduces herself as 'My name is Lizzy and I like to swing'." She laughed a little. "Richard and I adored her. She was so sweet and perfect.

"Two years after Lizzy was born, we had another child. A little boy named Matthew and, yes, he was named for my father."

Johnny's brow rose.

"He was about Lizzy's opposite. He was born four weeks premature and didn't leave the hospital for a little while. But soon he grew and was toddling everywhere after Richard."

"They sound like wonderful *kinner*. I'm sure my *kinner* would like to meet them."

She smiled and returned to her coffee. They sat in silence for a moment.

"So what caused you to return home?"

Mattie finished her coffee before setting down the mug and answering. "My husband. For the last several months, we've been drifting apart. He began working long hours at the office and came home late or sometimes not at all. It seemed like we could barely have a conversation without it ending in a fight. I did my best to hide the fact from the children but our marriage was just falling apart. Then I discovered why when I went to see Richard one day and found him sharing a moment with his secretary." She swallowed hard, then looked up at her cousin with glassy eyes. "I was so sick of all the lies that I decided to leave."

She turned away and blinked back her tears, struggling to keep her composure. "That's why I decided to take the children and return home."

"I'm really sorry for ya, Mattie. I hate to say it, but I feel that the *Englisch* oftentimes don't see marriage as important as our Plain folk do. It ain't meant to be torn asunder." He shook his head. "You should try to make amends with your husband. But if you can't, you know that your family would welcome you if you decided to stay. And *Der Herr* will take care of you and the *kinner*."

Mattie nodded and appreciated Johnny's support. She hated to admit it, but her cousin was right. "Thank you for inviting me, Johnny." She lifted a half smile. "Sorry for crying on your shoulder."

He waved a hand. "*Ach*, it was no problem. You know I'm here for you if you need to talk."

"I appreciate that. I've really enjoyed catching up with you."

"*Jah.* Me too."

Mattie smiled, reminiscing all the trouble she and her cousins had gotten into. They'd always been good friends – partners in crime.

"Should we head back?"

She nodded. "Sure."

They stood and headed to the front to pay for their meal, then out the door.

Mattie turned toward her car, not quite ready to leave her cousin's company. "Well, I'll do my best to make it to your parents' place on Christmas Eve."

"*Jah*, that will be *gut*. And bring your *kinner* too."

"I'll try. I'm sure they'll love getting to know your children."

Johnny grinned. "And who knows what kind of trouble they'll get into together."

Mattie laughed, imagining another set of mischief makers.

"Mattie?"

She turned at the voice behind her, and her heart froze like the puffs of air coming from her mouth. "Richard."

Just be sensible. Richard tried his best to think logically. Surely there was a reasonable explanation why Mattie had gone out to eat with another man.

Alone. Like a date.

And surely there had to be a reasonable explanation as to why Mattie was laughing with him and why they were discussing their children. And now in an embrace.

He felt like bashing the guy into the ground for trying to steal his wife's heart. *Not on my watch.*

"What are you doing here?" Mattie had gone pale, guilt surely plaguing her conscience.

"What am *I* doing here? No, the question is what are *you* doing here? There's a rift in our relationship and you run back home into the arms of *some* Amish guy?" He gestured angrily at the man.

Mattie's jaw gaped. "Wha–? Into–? What on earth are you talking about?"

"Don't play dumb, Mattie. It's quite obvious that you two were sharing a meal together. Alone. And then you go and tell Carson and Elisabeth that *I'm* the one having an affair!"

The Amish man stepped forward. "Are you saying Mattie and I are in a sinful relationship?"

Richard frowned at the man's hand on his wife's arm. Just who did this guy think he was? "Well, I don't know what *you* all call it, but it *my* book it's definitely sinful."

Mattie's cheeks flared with temper, a trait he had always thought attractive. "How could you? You...you make me so mad! Richard, just stop. Stop. I'm tired of your excuses," she snapped. "*I* am not the one tearing our marriage apart! You're the one who's been off rendezvousing with your secretary or whoever she is! So don't you dare start turning this on me!"

"There is nothing going on between me and my secretary, and that has nothing to do with the fact that *you* are here *alone* with another man!"

"Johnny's not–" She raked a hand through her hair. "Ugh! I refuse to discuss this here."

So it is that Johnny guy. Just as he'd suspected. "I'm as rational as a man can be when he finds his wife off on a date with another man!" He looked around and momentarily recoiled when he noticed a few bystanders eavesdropping on their conversation.

"You obviously have no desire to listen rationally!" Mattie turned and stalked toward her vehicle. "We're done, Richard. You can go ahead and return to New York! Without me and the children."

Richard hurried after her but she swiftly slid into her car and closed and locked the door. "Mattie, I'm not finished! We need to–"

Mattie turned the key and backed up her car, completely ignoring him. She started out of the parking lot and Richard turned to head back to his own vehicle.

"I think she's upset," the Amish man opened his mouth as he passed.

"Upset?" Richard threw a fist into the man's face, satisfaction cooling his temper. "Don't you ever come near my wife again!"

He jumped into his car and sped off, not quite sure where he was going.

This day hadn't turned out anything like he had expected.

NINE

*C*arson looked up when he heard the crunch of tires over the driveway's snow. Was that Richard's car? He strode over once it was parked. "Richard. What are you doing here?"

"Not you too. What, you want me to leave? Am I not welcome in my friend's home anymore?"

Carson's eyebrows rose in surprise.

Richard deflated, letting out a long breath. "Sorry, man, I didn't mean to snap at you."

"Apology accepted." Carson gave a smile, hoping to ease some of his friend's frustration. He obviously needed to vent. "What's going on, Richard?"

"Just about everything. I decided to come get Mattie, so I drove here to Pennsylvania from New York, not expecting to find my wife on a date with another man."

Carson winced. "Are you sure?"

"Uh, yeah. The two of them sharing a meal, laughing and talking, in an embrace." Richard nodded. "We argued, of course, and she drove off. I figured I'd come visit you. Get some moral support or something."

"Would you like to come inside, Richard?"

"I don't want to disturb Elisabeth and the kids."

"Don't worry, they went into town. It's just me and you."

"Sure then."

They tromped through the snow to the house and stepped inside, stamping the snow off their shoes onto the mat.

"Want anything to drink?"

"A beer sounds great."

Carson raised a brow. "You've started drinking?"

"No. Sorry. I'm just frustrated."

"I see."

"Nothing to drink. I'm fine." Richard plopped down onto the sofa.

Carson took a seat across from him. "Richard, do you sincerely want to get your marriage back?"

"Yes, I do."

"Good." Carson smiled. "I would like to try to help, but in order to do that, I need to know what is going on. Can you explain everything? From the very beginning, when you and Mattie first started having problems, to Mattie thinking you're having an affair, to you finding Mattie with some other guy."

Richard sighed, took a breath, and began.

Mattie couldn't believe the man she'd married. How could he have gone from her knight in shining armor who saved her from danger and bought her roses, to someone who confronted her and accused her of adultery at a public restaurant? She'd never been more humiliated – or angry.

Her last words to Richard rang in her mind, but she knew they were true. There was no way they could return to their happy marriage, not unless some severe changes were made. And she doubted Richard would be willing to make them.

She glanced down at her stomach and placed a hand over where her baby lay. "I'm so sorry," she whispered. "I'm sorry you have to grow up without a daddy."

"You mean to tell me that Johnny is only Mattie's cousin?" Richard's eyes grew wide.

"Yep. He's one of Jonathan Fisher's twins. From what Elisabeth has said, they were very close growing up and got into a lot of mischief together as teens," Carson explained.

"Oh, boy. Then I guess punching him in the face wasn't the best idea." He winced.

"You punched him in the face?" Richard didn't miss the bewilderment in his friend's tone.

"Regrettably." He frowned.

"I think it's safe to say that was probably not the best idea." Carson grimaced.

"It looks like I have an apology to make. Or two."

Carson nodded. "Perhaps we should pray."

"I think that's a good idea."

"Come on, boys, we need to bring all the stuff inside. Here, Lincoln, you take this bag for Mommy. And Jacob, you can take this one. You two are such good helpers." Elisabeth handed some things to her three- and four-year-old sons and scooted them toward the house. "I'll get baby Leah and the rest of the stuff."

She watched her boys hurry through the snow with grocery bags in hand and smiled. They were so cute. She turned and picked up Leah then gathered the remaining bags and her purse. She headed to the house to see Lincoln struggling to open the door while still carrying his bag. "Set the bag down and then try opening it," she suggested, wondering where Carson was. He surely would have come to help if he'd heard them.

Lincoln followed her instructions and quickly managed to open it, then turned to beam at her before stepping inside.

"Put the stuff in the kitchen, boys, and then go put your boots by the door." Elisabeth turned with Leah and started for the living room. She paused when she spotted Carson and Richard sitting on the sofa, their heads bowed in prayer. She smiled and went back to the boys. "When you two are done, why don't we all go take a nap?"

"But what about the candy canes?" Lincoln asked.

"Well, you're definitely not gonna have one just before bed. We can all have one with our hot cocoa after supper, all right?"

The four-year-old nodded in resignation.

"Okay, come on. Head up the stairs and go quietly. We don't want to wake up baby Leah if she's asleep."

Elisabeth followed the boys to their room and tucked them in. She checked on Benjamin and found him sleeping soundly. She brought little Leah to the bedroom she and Carson shared and set her down in her cradle. She sucked on her fingers contentedly, and Elisabeth moved to sit on the bed. If she had time, she'd have herself a nice nap too.

"Hey, babe."

Elisabeth turned to Carson and rose to meet him with a kiss. She pulled away after a few seconds. "Why is Richard here? Has something happened?"

"Yes. Richard came for help and advice and he explained everything. He isn't doing what Mattie thinks he is," he said seriously.

She sighed. "Good. So what *is* going on?"

"I'll tell you when I have more time. Richard's waiting for me downstairs. But know that he is willing to do what he has to in order to fix his marriage. He's not giving up yet."

She smiled. "I'm very happy to hear that and I look forward to hearing everything. Do you need me to fix you guys something for lunch?"

"No, we're fine, sweetheart. You can just lie down and rest. We can handle it."

"I still need to put the groceries away though."

"No, you don't. I'll get it. You just take a nap and relax."

"But–"

Carson raised a brow and took a step closer. "Do I need to convince you, wife?"

Elisabeth glanced up at his gorgeous eyes and couldn't help a furtive lick of her lips. "I wish you would," she whispered.

He grinned and leaned down for a knee-quaking kiss. After a few tantalizing moments, he pulled up and let out a breath. "I would love to, but Richard's waiting for me. He's probably already wondering where I am."

"I'm sure he'd understand."

"Don't tempt me." Carson gave her a quick kiss and started for the door. "Now you do as I say and take a nap, you hear?"

"Yes, Daddy," she teased.

He smiled and shut the door behind him.

Elisabeth lay back on her bed with her eyes wide open. She was dying for everything to be straightened out. She couldn't bear to see her best friend in a messy divorce. If Richard wasn't cheating on Mattie, they could surely figure it all out and get back together, right? At least she certainly hoped so.

TEN

$\mathcal{M}$attie huffed as she glanced down at her phone. Part of her hoped the call would be from Richard; the other part was livid and never wanted to speak with him again. She recognized the number.

Pastor? Why would the pastor be calling her?

She regrettably answered the call. "Hello?"

"Mattie, is this you?"

"Yes, it is."

"This is Pastor Bill. I'm sorry to bother you, Mattie, but I haven't been able to get a hold of your husband," the pastor explained. "It's not too urgent or anything. I just wanted to let Richard know that he left a few things here at the house. Margaret found his pillow in the guest bedroom and a towel. And he also forgot his Bible here."

"At *your* house?"

"Yes, ma'am. Margaret or I could stop by the house and drop them off for him. I'm sure he's been missing his Bible."

"Oh. Well, we're out of town right now." Mattie scratched her head, still perplexed by the pastor's words.

"If you could just let Richard know, I would appreciate it." The pastor paused. "By the way, Mattie, how are you doing?"

"I'm sorry. I really can't talk right now." She rushed through her words. "If I talk to Richard, I'll let him know you called."

"Thank you, Mattie. I also wanted to let you know that you and Richard are in our prayers."

"Okay. Uh, thank you. Goodbye." She clicked off the phone as quickly as she could. Mattie felt rude by her abruptness, but she wasn't ready for a sermon on divorce at the moment.

She tossed her cell phone onto the bed and stared at it as though it were a peculiar object. *Richard's things are at Pastor Bill's house?* The thought made absolutely no sense.

"Mattie!" Her thoughts were quickly interrupted by her mother's call from the bottom of the stairs. "Elisabeth's here."

Mattie rushed to the window and looked out. Odd. *Elisabeth's here alone?*

She checked on the children, who were contently playing in their room, then hurried down the stairs so as not to keep her friend waiting. Elisabeth and her mother were immersed in small talk when she reached the kitchen.

She smiled. "Lis. What a pleasant surprise."

"We need to talk."

Mattie's eyes met her friend's. She hadn't discussed her quarrel with Richard with anyone yet. Had Elisabeth heard about it through the grapevine already? "Okay. Let's take a walk?"

"Sure," her friend replied.

Mattie turned to her mother. "Will you keep an eye on the kids for me? They should be fine. I just checked on them before I came down. They were playing in Rebekah's room."

Her mother nodded with a smile.

"Let's walk in the woods?" Mattie suggested. She'd always loved this part of her parents' property and had missed it the most while living in the city.

Elisabeth followed her lead. "How have you been?"

"Oh, where to start! Well, Johnny and I went out for breakfast yesterday."

Her friend nodded, listening intently.

"What a mess. Richard showed up and he actually thought that Johnny and I were out on a date! Can you believe that? Oh, I was so mad at him. Later, I found out that Richard hit poor Johnny in the face!" She clenched her hands together and took a deep breath, attempting to control her anger. "And I–" Pain tore through her middle section and she immediately doubled over.

"Mattie, what's wrong?"

She struggled to breathe and tears pricked her eyes. "I think it's the baby!"

Richard truly believed it would all work out. Hearing Carson's support and now knowing that there was nothing beyond friendship going on between his wife and Johnny Fisher, he had almost no doubt on the matter. He and Mattie just had to talk and everything would come into place.

Thank You, God, for helping me figure all of this out. Please let Mattie hear me out and restore our marriage. I'm so sorry for drifting away from You. Please help me get back on track and help Mattie to-

His phone rang, cutting off his prayer, and he dug it out of his pocket to see who it was.

"Elisabeth?"

"Richard, I need you at the hospital right now." Alarm laced her tone.

"Why? What's happened? Is it Carson?"

"No. It's Mattie."

Dread squeezed his heart.

"What's wrong?"

"She's had strong cramping."

"What does that mean?"

"It means she's about to lose the baby."

"Baby?"

"Yes. She's pregnant, Richard. About nine weeks along. I went over to see her today and she started spotting. I got her to the hospital as quickly as I could. I don't know much about these things, Richard, but it's not good. There's a really good chance she could lose the baby."

He couldn't breathe. He was still trying to process the fact that his wife was expecting a child. "She- she's pregnant?" he reiterated.

"Yes, Richard. And if I wasn't so worried right now, I'd offer you congratulations."

"I-I'll be there as soon as I can, Elisabeth." He almost hung up then realized he didn't know where to go. "Wait! Give me the address to the hospital so I can put it in my GPS." He quickly jotted down the information.

Richard hung up and sat in silence for a stunned moment.

Mattie was expecting a baby! His baby. But something was wrong and she might lose the baby. Not good at all.

He grabbed his keys and sprinted out of his hotel room, praying the entire way to the car.

Carson let out a breath as he spotted Richard rushing to the hospital entrance.

"Carson! How's Mattie? Do you know what's happened?"

"All I know is she's in room 201. Elisabeth said I should wait here for you."

Richard continued to the elevator and pushed the button. They waited for a moment. "You know, this is taking too long. Where's the stairs?"

"I have no idea, Richard. We should probably just wait."

The elevator opened a second later, for which Carson was grateful. He didn't doubt Richard would have charged the first hospital employee he saw and demanded that they direct him to the stairs if it hadn't. They stepped inside and Carson noticed his friend's fingers agitatedly drumming against his leg as they ascended.

Finally it came to a halt on the second floor and they stepped off. Richard practically ran to the waiting room and Carson hurried to catch up with him.

Elisabeth was waiting for them.

"How is she? Do you know how bad it is? Will the baby live?"

"I don't know, Richard. I haven't seen her since we first arrived."

"How did this all happen?"

Elisabeth quickly explained what she had told Carson. They had been walking and Mattie began cramping.

Richard sighed in frustration. "Why didn't she tell me she was expecting a baby?"

"Did you expect her to?" Elisabeth asked. "With how things have been going between you two lately?"

"Yes. Well, I guess not. I don't know. But this is really important. I don't understand why she wouldn't tell me."

"She saw no reason to. She thought you were having an affair. She thought you had rejected her. She probably didn't think you'd care."

"I can't believe she would think that. I've always cared." He ran a hand through his hair. "Do you know anything about this sort of thing at all?"

Elisabeth shook her head, her eyes misting. Carson put his arm around her. "I'm sorry, Richard, but it isn't good. All I know is that spotting is usually a sure sign of a miscarriage."

Richard sank into a chair and covered his face with his hands. "Oh, God, watch over them. Help them and please, don't let our baby die. Or Mattie. Please."

Carson and Elisabeth sat beside their friend and joined him in prayer. If anyone could help Mattie and their unborn child, it was the Saviour of the universe.

ELEVEN

"*I*s someone here for Mattie Greene?"

Richard jumped at the voice and hurried to the nurse, Carson and Elisabeth following closely behind him. "I'm her husband. How is she?"

"She's resting now. It was a close call. She nearly miscarried, but as far as we can tell, the fetus is all right. For now." The nurse looked pointedly at Richard. "She will need to be on strict bedrest."

Richard frowned. "For how long?"

"Just to be on the safe side, we want Mrs. Greene on bed rest until at least the twenty weeks mark, with no physical exertion or emotional upset of any kind. She'll need to see the doctor again in about a month from now."

Relief hit Richard so strong, he had to blink tears from his eyes. "Thank God they're all right. May I see her?"

"When would it be safe for her to return home?" Elisabeth asked at the same time.

"We would like her to stay overnight at the least, but there will be no visiting during that time. Right now rest is what she needs."

"Thank you."

The nurse nodded and left the waiting room.

Carson clapped a hand on his friend's shoulder. "She'll be just fine."

Richard nodded, eyes bright. "I can't believe I have to wait until tomorrow to see her."

"I'm afraid it'll be longer than that."

He turned to Elisabeth. "Why?"

"The nurse said no upset of any kind. I hate to tell you this, Richard, but if Mattie sees you, she could lose the baby. Stress is your baby's worst enemy right now. You've been the main source of Mattie's frustration the last few weeks. You should probably wait."

Richard opened his mouth to protest.

"I think she's right, buddy," Carson said. "Right now, it's better for Mattie if you aren't there. I'd give her a week of rest before you go talk to her."

Elisabeth nodded. "At least."

Richard sighed, frustration evident in his tone. "I'll do my best."

Mattie sat on the small chair in her room and attempted to concentrate on her book. After a few moments of switching between thinking and following the characters, she laid her novel to the side. There was no point in it. Her own world was too crazy for her to distract herself with someone else's.

Richard.

She was still trying to fathom Pastor Bill's phone call. So Richard hadn't been living with his secretary as she'd assumed, and he wasn't staying at the office. He'd been sleeping at the pastor's house instead. So he'd been dating his secretary while staying with the pastor? What a hypocrite. And Pastor Bill most likely had no idea.

She sighed. It seemed impossible for them to get back together. She wished they could simply talk things out but apparently that wasn't going to happen. Not when everything turned into an argument. And she had no desire to be with an angry Richard, especially if he was inclined to use force like he had with Johnny.

How had everything turned out so wrong?

Richard sat on the edge of the hotel bed with the remote and flicked the television on. He aimlessly flipped through the channels and baffled that, with over fifty channels, there was still nothing good to watch. He quickly turned the television off again.

Of course, the fact that he felt like a caged animal didn't help his frustration. If only he could see Mattie. There were so many things he wanted to tell her, things he wanted to clear up and make right.

But he'd do what was best for Mattie – and their baby. She'd been pregnant for nine weeks and hadn't mentioned *anything* to him. That was something he was still trying to wrap his mind around. Under normal circumstances, this situation would have caused an argument. But Richard had to keep his cool, no matter how much he wished to voice his frustration over his wife's disregard for his paternal right to know. How could she think that keeping a secret of this magnitude was acceptable – even if they were at odds?

Expressing his ambivalent feelings toward his wife and her behavior would prove to be a feat in itself. He'd have to address the situation delicately, if he were to approach the subject at all. Perhaps he would let it slide for now. After all, the most important thing was that Mattie and the baby were alive and healthy.

He hated to think that he could be the cause for Mattie's emotional upset. Her emotions had always been somewhat volatile, or as his sister had succinctly put it, Mattie had a tendency to be a drama queen at times. But he often chalked that up to her being a woman. Weren't most women emotional?

Richard sighed and reached for the Gideon's Bible he'd been using as a substitute since he arrived at the hotel. Thankfully, they still provided them in this establishment. It was the one thing he'd always been thankful for, when staying at hotels. The faithful placement of Gideon Bibles was something that, too often, was taken for granted. How many lives had been changed because of them? he now wondered.

While he was appreciative of their presence, there were drawbacks. The main disadvantage of using a Bible that didn't belong to him, was not being able mark the passages that held special meaning and writing notes in the margins. He could've kicked himself for forgetting to bring his own Bible. He felt out of place without it. For the life of him, he couldn't remember where he'd left it.

He turned to the place he'd been reading. It seemed like the Bible always contained the answers he needed, although oftentimes the answers were not what he *wanted* to hear. Sometimes his mind conflicted with the words on the page and he'd have to make a conscious decision to forfeit his own will and agree with God.

As he now read through First Peter, chapter three, he nodded in agreement of how women should conduct themselves. His eyes landed on verse seven. *Likewise, ye husbands, dwell with them according to knowledge, giving honour unto the wife, as unto the weaker vessel, and being heirs together of the grace of life; that your prayers be not hindered.*

Richard briefly pondered the words, then continued.

Finally, be ye all of one mind, having compassion one of another, love as brethren, be pitiful, be courteous: Not rendering evil for evil, or railing for railing: but contrariwise blessing; knowing that ye are thereunto called, that ye should inherit a blessing. For he that will love life, and see good days, let him refrain his tongue from evil, and his lips that they speak no guile: Let him eschew evil, and do good; let him seek peace, and ensue it. For the eyes of the Lord are over the righteous, and his ears are open unto their prayers:

Richard bowed his head, thoroughly humbled. He prayed aloud, "God, please help me to be the husband You want me to be – the man that my wife and children need. Forgive me for falling short so many times. Help me to honor Mattie. Give me the compassion she needs and help me to refrain my tongue from evil. Let me speak only words of blessing and not strife. God, we need peace in our home – peace that only You can give. Please hear my prayer, Lord. May You receive all the glory. I ask these things in the name of my precious Saviour, Jesus, whose birth we will be celebrating in just a few days. God, if You will restore my marriage and save my baby, that will be the best Christmas gift I could ever ask for. Thank You. Amen."

TWELVE

*I*t had been a week.

Richard was done waiting.

He tried to think of how he was going to explain things to Mattie. Her getting upset was the last thing she needed. It would be best for her and the baby's health to stay calm. So he would simply tell her everything quietly and rationally. *Yes, that will work*, he decided as he drove to her parents' house.

And that was another thing. He was probably going to meet Mattie's parents today. What would they think of him? Surely Mattie had told them what was going on in their relationship. What was their perception of him? Most likely, they'd already formed a biased opinion based on the knowledge they'd acquired from their daughter. Which was undoubtedly *not* the best thing.

How would he be received? *Would* he be received? Did they already hate him? What would he do if they didn't let him in? He shouldn't use force, should he? No, that would just make things worse. But he *had* to talk to his wife.

What else could he do? He'd tried to call her – multiple times. He'd thought of writing her a letter, but who knows if they'd burn it before Mattie even saw it. If they harbored hatred toward him, that could be a possibility.

No, he'd go see her. Visiting in person was, no doubt, his best chance of seeing his wife.

Richard sighed. *Dear Lord, please guide me as I visit the Riehls' residence. Please let Mattie's parents accept me and allow me to talk with her. I pray that our conversation will be calm and that I will be able to explain so Mattie can hear the truth. Please let her be willing to return to our marriage, God. I pray that You will just have Your hand over this day, Lord. Don't let the devil prosper. In Jesus' name, amen.*

As his GPS directed him into a long driveway, he inhaled deeply. *This must be it.* He continued up to the house and spotted Lizzy and someone, who he guessed was Mattie's father, playing by the swings. He parked his car and stepped out.

"Daddy!"

He turned at his daughter's voice just before she threw herself at him. Tears pricked his eyes as she squeezed him into her arms. "Hi, Lizzy."

She pulled back and he lifted her into his arms. "I knew you were gonna come, Daddy! Momma said you weren't, but I knew you would!" She buried her face into his neck, her nose cold against his skin.

"I couldn't spend Christmas without my Busy Lizzy! Of course, I had to come. And I plan to stay for a while too, if your

Momma will let me." He set his daughter back onto the snow-packed ground.

Lizzy nodded happily. "She will. I know she will. Mommy cries when you're not here."

The older man approached them. "Lizzy, why don't you go inside and see what your grandma is doing. Your father and I need to talk."

"No!" Lizzy shook her head adamantly and clung to Richard's pant leg. "I want to stay with Daddy!"

Richard crouched down next to her and spoke softly but firmly. "Do as your grandfather says, Lizzy."

"But I miss you, Daddy!" Her eyes filled with tears and she hiccupped.

"It's okay, Lizzy. I'm not going to leave. You go on into the house now."

She nodded tearfully.

"I love you, Lizzy."

"I love you too, Daddy."

Lizzy turned and slowly walked to the house, glancing back every few seconds as though to be sure he was still there. Richard gave her an encouraging nod and she finally entered the house with a little wave. He quickly swiped at his eyes before straightening to meet his father-in-law's gaze.

The man surveyed him observantly before speaking. "I hope you care for Matilda as much as you care for Lizzy."

Matilda? Richard frowned, then realized who the man spoke of. "Mattie." Richard nodded. "Yes, I do. Even more so."

The man watched him thoughtfully for a moment. "I am Matthew Riehl, Matilda's father." He extended a hand.

Richard shook it. "I'm Richard Greene, Mattie's husband."

Matthew nodded. "Tell me why you are here, Richard Greene."

"To talk to my wife."

"To talk to her or to argue with her?"

"Just talk, hopefully."

"And what are you planning to talk about?"

For a moment Richard felt like telling the man it was none of his business and he had the right to speak with his wife whenever he wished, but he knew the disrespectful statement would not be well received. "I would like to explain everything to her and to tell her I have no desire to let this be the end of our marriage."

Matthew nodded again. "I, too, do not wish to see my daughter divorced. But Mattie believes you have been unfaithful to her, and that is not an accusation made lightly. I'd appreciate an explanation."

"I would really like to speak with Mattie about it."

"I understand. But as she is currently under *my* care, I will do my best to keep her from any and all harm, emotionally and physically."

Richard didn't miss his father-in-law's accusatory tone. "With all due respect, sir, I have no intention of harming my wife."

"From what my daughter's told me, I find that hard to believe."

"Listen, Mr. Riehl. I know you care for your daughter. But I love her even more. What Mattie believes about me is untrue. I'd like to clear things up between us, but I cannot do that if I don't have access to her."

"Are you saying you *have not* had an inappropriate relationship with another woman?"

"No." *Wait a minute. What was the question?* "I mean, yes. Of course, I haven't had a relationship with another woman. I told you already. I love my wife."

"Yet you leave her and the children alone for weeks? In the big city, where all sorts of mischief takes place?" Her father raised a condescending brow.

His words pierced Richard's heart. Is that what he'd done? Left his wife and children open to attack from enemies – both physical and spiritual? He frowned, now ashamed of his thoughtless actions.

Her father drove his point home. "I don't know if I'd call that love."

"Please, Mr. Riehl." Richard raked a hand through his hair. How could he get through to this man? "Okay, I admit that I haven't done everything right. I'm not perfect and I don't expect I'll ever be. But I'm trying here. I wouldn't have come all this way to get Mattie and the kids if I didn't love them."

"I see."

Richard sighed and waited patiently for Mattie's father to acquiesce.

Matthew frowned. "I will see if she cares to see you."

Richard blew out a breath as he watched Mattie's father stride toward the house. *Okay, God. I guess I deserved that. Did You just put Mattie's father in my path to toughen my character?* He needed to regain his calm demeanor if he was to see Mattie soon. At the moment, he was too worked up. It had been a while since his patience had been tested to this extent.

Richard bent down, grasped a handful of clean snow, and rubbed it on his face. He shivered from the freezing temperature of the ice, but it forced his mind to momentarily think of something else.

Was Matthew talking to Mattie even now? If so, what was he saying? And how was she responding?

As the minutes ticked by, it seemed like he'd been forgotten. *God, please give me a chance to talk to her.*

He turned when he heard the door creak open. Mattie's father strode toward him purposefully, and his stomach clenched in anticipation of his response. He couldn't read Matthew's expression.

Mattie's father nodded. "She has agreed to speak with you."

THIRTEEN

*R*ichard breathed deeply and followed his father-in-law into the house. Lizzy beamed at him from the table where she sat eating a snack, and he tossed her a wink and a smile. He continued up the stairs until Matthew came to a stop in front of a bedroom door.

"This is Mattie's room. You may go in and speak with her." He shot a pointed look in Richard's direction. "You may not upset her. If you do, you will not be welcome back into this house. Do you understand?"

"I do, sir. Thank you." Richard tarried by the door and studied his father-in-law, who stood sentinel.

The man gave him a questioning look.

So he had to spell it out. Richard frowned. "May I speak with her *alone*, please?"

A twinkle lit the man's eye then quickly vanished. "Oh yes, of course." He turned and started down the stairs.

Richard rested his hand on the doorknob, whispered a quick prayer, and then opened the door.

Of all the items on Mattie's mental list of things to do, seeing her unfaithful husband ranked pretty close to the bottom. Yes, she still loved him. But she was uncertain whether she could ever trust him again.

The only reason she'd agreed to see him was to appease her father. He had insisted she give Richard a chance to explain his side of the story. She valued her father's advice *now*. Although they didn't agree on everything, they'd gotten along surprisingly well since she'd returned. Out of respect for her father, and a smidgen of curiosity, she agreed to talk to Richard. Hesitantly. And since added stress wouldn't help the baby any, she decided not to protest either.

Richard currently stood by the door, observing her as though she were an old acquaintance he hadn't seen in years, and he was unsure of what to say first. A silent moment passed as she waited patiently for him to say or do something.

"Hello, Mattie. I hope you're feeling better," he spoke the words softly.

"What did you come here for, Richard?" She fought to keep the bitterness out of her voice.

She expected her wayward husband to retaliate with a terse remark. Instead, she noticed that he fought the immediate response that flew to his lips. She frowned, but her respect for him increased.

"I-I came to set things straight between us, Mattie. I don't want to lose you."

Mattie sneered. "Right."

He ventured forward a step, a sheepish expression filled his features. "I'll answer *any* questions you have, but first off, I want you to know I'm *not* the complete jerk that you think I am."

"Really?" Mattie raised a brow. "And I'm supposed to believe that?"

"I haven't been unfaithful to you, Mattie," he insisted, his voice strained. "Not once. I promise."

"Then explain to me why you're away from home so often. Why do you no longer have time for me and the kids? Why did I come to your office and find you holding hands with your secretary?" Mattie tried to calm her breathing. She was getting worked up and that was not a good thing.

"I was away from home so much because I was called in to work. We had a legal emergency. I didn't want to alarm you about the dire situation we were dealing with. One of the companies our firm was involved with was discovered to have embezzled funds, millions of dollars, from several clients. Because of the relationship between their company and ours, the business was in jeopardy. My boss called me in to work longer hours as we all tried to combat the claims against the company. Because of legal issues, I was not at liberty to discuss the issues at hand.

"I spent as much time with you and the children as I could. When I didn't come home, I stayed the night at Pastor Bill's place. I was trying to get help for our marriage. You refused to go to counseling, so I went alone. His place was closer to the office and, honestly, I didn't want to come home to another argument. I was exhausted. And I knew that the children didn't need to hear us fighting all the time."

Mattie tried to process everything he'd said. "Oh, so you're saying it was *my* fault that you didn't come home."

"No, that's not what I'm saying. Please, just stop assuming things." Richard's fist closed and then released.

Mattie took a deep breath and attempted to keep her voice level. "What do you expect when I visit you at your office and you're holding hands with another woman?"

"I told you that I could explain that, if you'd just hear me out. The only reason I was holding hands with my secretary is because we were *praying*. For you and me and *our* marriage. Mattie, she is a godly Christian woman, with whom I happen to pray from time to time. She's also married herself and has a baby boy."

"And you expect me to believe that?" Mattie wanted to believe his words, but she wasn't ready to accept them just yet. She needed more proof of his alleged innocence.

"You can speak with any of them if you want – my boss, my secretary, Pastor. I'm sure they'd all be willing to give you their side of the story." He rubbed the stubble on his chin. "If it makes a difference, I'll even fire my secretary if that's what you'd like. There's nothing in this world more important to me than you."

"I don't want you to fire her, but I'm not fond of the idea of you holding hands with another woman – even if it is to pray."

"Done. I won't do it again."

Richard approached the bed and took her hand. "I love you, Mattie Greene, and I would never purposely do anything to destroy our marriage."

Her eyes misted and she met his gaze. "Then why has *everything* been so difficult? How come we can hardly even talk anymore without it becoming an argument?"

"Pastor Bill explained to me why he thinks we're having so much trouble – lack of communication. Carson basically said the same thing. Somewhere along the line, we've disconnected. With me being away from home so often, it causes a rift in our relationship. And then when we talk, we're both uptight and lonely and feel betrayed because we have physical and emotional needs that don't get met.

"Neglecting church doesn't help either, and I realize that's my fault, as the spiritual leader of our home. Perhaps your change in hormones with this new little one of ours could also be contributing to the stress. When we don't communicate, or *mis*communicate, things aren't properly understood and we end up arguing. And then we let *fear* fester in our minds and come to absolutely ridiculous conclusions – like me having an affair with my secretary and you running off with your *cousin*." He frowned.

She couldn't help a small smile. "Did Elisabeth tell you about Johnny?"

"Carson did, in fact. I wish I'd known before I went and made an idiot of myself." He grinned ruefully.

She chuckled a little. "I think we need to come up with a new rule: assume nothing."

"That sounds like a plan." He lifted a brief smile then turned serious. "So what does this mean for us, Mattie? Will you forgive me for all the foolish mistakes I've made?"

Mattie perceived the trepidation in Richard's eyes, and her heart warmed at his open vulnerability. He truly did love her like he claimed. She knew that if she rejected him, she'd break his heart. How could she help but love him?

She nodded. "This means we have to wait about ten weeks before we can go back home."

He sighed in relief. "Do you think there's room in this place for the two of us? Staying at the hotel all alone will get awfully lonely."

"You'll need to discuss *that* with my father, but I'll put in a good word for you," she teased.

Richard's face split into a grin and he leaned down and pressed his lips against hers. She reached up and held him there. *This* was the man she'd fallen in love with.

Now that she was back in his arms, she never wanted to let him go.

FOURTEEN

Elisabeth sipped on her wassail and turned to Carson. "It's too bad Mattie and Richard couldn't make it to the Christmas party. I hate to see them miss out."

"Yep, it's unfortunate for them," Carson sympathized, "but at least they're together now."

"I have an idea. Let's bring the party to them." Jonathan Fisher's face beamed.

"Won't that be too upsetting for Mattie?" Carson interjected.

"How could bringing good tidings of great joy be upsetting? If anything, it'll lift her spirits," Jonathan reasoned.

"You're right. Let's do it." Elisabeth smiled.

"We'll sing Christmas hymns at their door," Susanna Fisher suggested.

"I've always loved Christmas caroling. She'll feel so lucky," Annie Hostettler beamed.

"Should we call Matthew and Maryanna and warn them?" Elisabeth reached for her phone.

"No way, they'll love a good surprise," Jonathan said.

"You mean, you'll love seeing the bewildered look on Mary-anna's face when we all show up!" Susie smiled.

"You know me well, *schatzi*." Jonathan winked at his wife.

"But Luke and Brianna haven't showed up yet. Should we wait for them?" Elisabeth suggested. "Who else isn't here yet?"

"Luke and Brianna are always late!" Elisabeth's brother, Jacob, smiled at his wife. "*Ain't so*, Rachel?"

Rachel nodded. "*Jah*, but they should be here any minute. You know how it is with a new little one in the house. It's not that easy to just get up and go."

Everyone near nodded in agreement.

"Let's all bundle up and go in the sleighs! Or maybe our *Englisch* friends will take us?" Jonathan asked.

"I'm not too sure we have room for everyone, but we can take the smallest ones to keep them out of the weather," Carson suggested.

"*Jah*," Jonathan agreed. "Or, we can leave them home with Bishop Judah. I'm sure *Grossmammi* Lydia won't mind a few extra little ones to watch."

"Gideon and I can stay too," Esther Fisher, Jonathan's mother, volunteered.

Carson turned from the window. "It looks like Luke and Brianna just showed up. I'll run out and tell them not to unhitch."

"Let's go!" Jonathan announced, then threw his arm around his brother-in-law's shoulder. "Hey, Josh. What do you say if we greet Matt with a snowball or two?" He raised his eyebrows twice and mischief flickered in his eyes.

"I'm in!" Joshua Hostettler grinned.

"Is that singing?" Mattie sat up and listened.

"You're not getting up," Richard warned. "Bed rest, remember?"

"But, Richard. It's Christmas Eve! And I thought I heard singing outside." Being cooped up in her room was beginning to grate on her nerves.

Richard arose and moved to look out the window. "It looks like Carson and Elisabeth and a bunch of Amish people."

"Really?" Mattie perked up.

"I think they're here for you." Richard grinned and opened the window slightly.

Mattie smiled as familiar voices wafted into the room. Silent Night in the original tongue resounded off the walls. It was the first time this season actually felt like the Christmases she'd been used to. She closed her eyes and blinked back tears. Only her friends and family in Paradise would do something so thoughtful.

"Mattie, you should have seen *Dat* and *Onkel* Josh get your *vatter*!" Judah Fisher smiled.

Mattie gasped. "What happened?"

"When everyone was singing outside your window, *Dat* and *Onkel* Josh knocked on the door. When your *vatter* answered, they hid. He went back inside and they knocked again. This time they hid too – I think your *vatter* thought it was the *kinner*. Then your *vatter* walked out and both *Dat* and *Onkel* Josh hopped out of the shrubs and ambushed your *vatter* with snowballs!"

Mattie smiled. "No way."

"Yep, and your *vatter* went right after them, chasing them down the lane!" Johnny added, laughing.

"Oh, I wish I could have seen that!" Mattie smiled at Richard and explained, "My father and two uncles were the best of friends growing up, and they have always pulled pranks on each other. I guess that's where I got my mischievous streak from."

"We," JJ reminded.

"Yeah." Mattie smiled, then noticed two young ladies standing in the doorway behind them. "Is that–?"

"Oh, yeah." The twins nodded and grasped the hands of the young women. They approached Mattie's bed. "These are our wives, Sarah Ann and Ellie."

"Nice to meet you." Mattie smiled. "I'm glad JJ found someone to straighten them out," she teased.

Mattie turned to Richard. "I don't think you've properly met my cousins." She gestured toward the twins. "Richard, this is Johnny and Judah. JJ, meet my husband, Richard."

He stepped forward and shook the young men's hands.

"Which one of you is Johnny?" Richard lifted a brow.

One of the twins lifted his hand. "That'd be me." He grinned.

"Sorry about punching you in the face. I'm afraid I made a terrible first impression." Richard grimaced.

"Oh, no. Don't feel bad. That was probably the best impression you could have given me. It showed that you really do love your wife. Man, if I thought my wife was seeing another man, I just might have done the same thing." He shook his hand and smiled. "No hard feelings."

"Thanks."

"I'm just glad that you and Mattie are still together and you've worked out your problems."

Richard moved a little closer to his wife's side and smiled. "Yeah. Me, too." He grasped her hand. "God is good."

"Mattie, how can we make this Christmas special for you?" Judah raised a brow.

"You already have." She smiled.

"Is there nothing else we can do?" Johnny asked. "I can get you some more hot cocoa."

Mattie truly did have the best of family and friends. "Thanks, Johnny, but I'm fine. There is one thing, though. Could we sing *O Holy Night*?"

Johnny looked at Judah. "Do we know that one?"

Judah nodded. "Think so." He rushed to the top of the stairs. "Hey, everyone! Mattie would like for us to sing *O Holy Night*. Who knows it?" He paused and Mattie guessed some of them raised their hands. She was quite certain Carson and Elisabeth knew the song. "Okay. *Onkel* Josh, will you be our *Vorsinger*?"

Her uncle's lone voice rang out and the others quickly joined in. Mattie sang along, with eyes closed, picturing the words in her mind. Mary, expecting a baby, just as she was, and Joseph in a stable awaiting the birth of the coming King. Angels and shepherds proclaiming the Messiah was born. And finally, she pictured herself, falling on her knees before her precious Saviour and worshipping the God who not only brought her and Richard back together, but gave His life to save the world from sin.

It was indeed a holy night, and this Christmas was one she would never forget.

For God so loved the world, that he gave his only begotten Son, that whosoever believeth in him should not perish, but have everlasting life. John 3:16 KJV

The End

What did you think of the book? We'd love to hear your thoughts! Your honest review would be an immense blessing to other potential readers and to the author.

Many thanks!

Would you like to be one of the first to hear about new releases? Do you love giveaways? Sign up for our monthly newsletter here at www.jebspredemann.com

If you'd like to purchase a paperback copy (or two) of *Christmas in Paradise* (paperback available Winter 2015) for a friend or to add to your own library, please visit our website for purchase links: www.jebspredemann.com

Other books in this series:

Englisch on Purpose

Amish by Accident http://amzn.to/1EbXbk5

Other ***Christmas*** offerings from **Blessed Publishing**:

A Christmas of Mercy J.E.B. Spredemann

As Christmas draws near, Katrina Thompson looks forward to the birth of her first grandchild. But when the blessed event digs up the discovery of her buried criminal past, Officer Love feels duty-bound to report the wrongdoing. The Amish community of Paradise has long since forgiven Katrina for her past mistakes, but will she receive mercy at the hands of the law?

A Christmas to Remember Michelynn Christy

Excerpt from Michelynn Christy's
A Christmas to Remember:

ONE

I can't believe I'm doing this! Samantha frantically ran the brush through her hair. There were a bazillion things she needed to pack before heading out to Mom's. Clothing, toiletries, camera, and the gifts. The ones she hadn't even purchased yet.

Why *would* she have needed to purchase gifts if she hadn't planned on returning home for Christmas? No. The plan was to spend an exciting Christmas weekend with Tammy and Jill. And that *had* been the plan until yesterday. Why couldn't her roommates have informed her sooner that they were going home for Christmas? But the brink of Christmas Eve? Well, that was just fine and dandy! It was a wonderful plan for them – they were sisters. They had each other. What would she do now? Spend Christmas all alone? Not gonna happen.

A quick phone call to Mom and a new plan had been forged. Of course, now she'd have to pay triple for the airfare. And purchase gifts. *There goes my spring break.* Oh well, it was Christmas. And she was determined to make it a memorable one.

"Ma'am, would you like a blanket or pillow?"

Samantha glanced up at the flight attendant. "Both would be great. Thanks."

She gladly took the items from the flight attendant's hands and immediately wrapped the blanket around her. Maybe a nap would relieve some of her anxiety.

This would be her first time home since she'd left for college nearly a year and a half ago. Leaving home had been rough. And if she were honest with herself, deep inside she really didn't even want to go away to college. But she had to. She had to get away from *him*.

Travis.

He'd first asked her out for a date in high school. They'd met at a football game. He was rooting for the opposing team, so she assumed he attended their rival school. She'd been correct. He was a couple of years older and way out of her league, she'd thought.

Dating Travis would be a dream come true – and it was. They went out nearly every weekend and spent most of their free time together. Anyone could clearly see that she and Travis were in love. Many nights they'd talked about a future together. She often dreamt of the day she'd become his wife. He was all she'd ever wanted – handsome, thoughtful, caring...or so she'd thought.

I don't understand what went wrong. Even now, she fought back tears. Perhaps it wouldn't have been so bad if she hadn't given herself away to him. She'd always planned on waiting till marriage, of finding that perfect one. She was so sure they'd be married someday. He'd said he loved her.

He'd lied. And she'd been naïve enough to believe his words.

Everything was wonderful until a couple of months after graduation. That's when she got the dreaded text message. He wanted to break up. He thought it would be a good idea if they dated other people. Why would she want to date anyone else when she'd already found her perfect match?

Stinkin' liar. How could someone just throw away a two-year relationship? The coward could have at least broken up with her in person. But then he'd have to look her in the eye. He'd have to see the hurt on her face and the pain he'd caused.

She quickly brushed away the tear that slid down her cheek unbidden. Why was this still so difficult? It wasn't because he was good-looking, or because he had plenty of money. No, she was certain it was because she loved him with all her heart. She'd believed he was her soul mate – the one person in this world she was to cherish all her days. She'd given him *everything*, believing he was reciprocating her affections. But instead of her anticipated marriage proposal, Travis had dumped her like yesterday's garbage.

An ostentatious chortle brought her attention to a young man just beyond the empty seat beside her. His face was bright as he stared at the airline catalog in his hands. He glanced her way and noticed she'd been watching. How couldn't she? Chances are, all the passengers heard his jovial outburst.

"You've got to see this!" He handed the catalog to Samantha.

She glanced down at the advertisement and smiled. The front of the t-shirt for sale read 'Let's eat Grandma!' other than 'Let's eat, Grandma!'; the back read 'Punctuation saves lives'. She recalled seeing something like that on Facebook before, but apparently this was the first time this man had seen it.

Samantha nodded. "It's funny." She handed the catalog back to him.

"Sorry, if I bothered you." His forehead creased.

"Oh no, it's fine." A change of thought was welcome.

The man held out his hand. "My name's William."

She reluctantly shook his hand. She'd never been too keen on meeting strangers. "Samantha."

"Where're you going?" he asked.

Should she share her plans with a complete stranger? She eyed him covertly. By his jeans, raglan shirt, and baseball cap, she figured he was just a friendly all-American guy. She guessed him to be about twenty-five. "Fresno," she divulged. It wasn't *exactly* her destination, but that's the airport she'd be arriving at.

"Really? Me too. Do you have family there?"

"Yes. Well, not *in* Fresno. My parents live in a small town, not too far from there. How about you?"

"All my family's back East. I really hated to leave them right before the holidays, but my new employer called and requested that I come early. I guess they had an emergency and wanted me to help out."

"Where will you be working?"

"At a church. I'm their new youth pastor."

"Oh."

"Not your typical job, I know. But serving the youth is my passion. It's such a dynamic age – just between childhood and adulthood. It's a difficult time for many of them and I want to show them God's love and help them make wise decisions that can have a positive impact on the rest of their lives."

Yep, he was certainly excited about his new career.

A voice called over the intercom. "Please return to your seats and fasten your safety belts. We will be arriving in Fresno in approximately thirty minutes."

Samantha noticed a few passengers heading back to their seats.

"Do you attend church anywhere?" He grinned.

Samantha shook her head. "No."

"Well, if you're looking for a place to attend, you'll already know the youth pastor." He chuckled. "I don't know if you'd consider that a positive or a negative."

She smiled. This guy didn't seem anything like how she'd envisioned a pastor.

"Ooh, no response. That's never a good sign."

"No, it's just that...you're not anything like what I'd imagined a pastor to be."

He winced. "Is that a good thing or a bad thing?"

"Good, I think."

He wrote down an address and phone number on the back of a little booklet and handed it to her. "We'll be having a candlelight service at a quarter to midnight on Christmas Eve. You're welcome to join us."

She received the invitation from his hand and slipped it into her purse. "Thank you."

"So, do you have big plans for Christmas?"

"I've got dinner at my parents' house on Christmas Eve. The following morning, my extended relatives will come over for breakfast and we'll exchange gifts." In spite of the unpleasant memories of Travis, she was glad to be home. Truthfully, there was no place she'd rather be. "How about you?"

"Not quite sure. I'm staying with the pastor and his wife. He's an older gentleman, so I don't think they have any children at home. I don't know how they usually celebrate the holidays.

I have a feeling that they won't be doing too much, though. Part of the reason I'm starting my job early is because Pastor Marshall sprained his ankle. He has to wear a cast on his entire leg for at least six weeks."

"Oh no, that's terrible. Does that mean you'll be preaching?"

He chuckled. "I hope not. The congregation might just get up and leave, if I did."

"But I thought—"

"I'm just the youth pastor. I don't mind being in front of a group of young folks, but looking out at adults scares me to death. We had to preach before a congregation several times in Bible College. That's when I determined I'm more comfortable with young people." He smiled. "I have to keep reminding myself of the verse 'For God hath not given us a spirit of fear…'"

"What will you be doing at the church then?"

"I imagine I'll be driving Pastor Marshall around to make his usual visits. And I'll help out wherever I'm needed." He shrugged.

"Even if it means preaching?" She raised a brow.

"If they ask me to, I will. But I'm hoping they won't ask. They have an assistant pastor and I'm guessing he fills in when needed."

"I hate public speaking too."

This time, the pilot's voice spoke. "Flight crew, prepare for landing."

"It looks like we're about to arrive. Well, Samantha, it was a pleasure meeting you." He smiled. "Hopefully, we'll see each other again sometime."

"It was nice meeting you too." Was it really time to go? A part of her wished she could have more time to get to know William. He was so friendly and easy to talk to.

Want to read more? Just $0.99 in ebook format.

A SPECIAL THANK YOU

To our fabulous **Street Team**, who help us 'Sprede the Word'

To **Heather**, our gifted paperback formatter at
Art & Design Studios

To **Lucinda**, our talented Smashwords formatter

To **Brandi**, the best VA ever

www.ingramcontent.com/pod-product-compliance
Lightning Source LLC
Chambersburg PA
CBHW052005170626
46808CB00007B/2791